TO HAVE AND TO HOLD

By

P. J. Usher

Dedication

Pam Usher is an artist and writer living in the north west of England. This novel was inspired by a visit to Quarry Bank Mill an old cotton mill near Styal Manchester. This book is dedicated to the men women and children who worked in the cotton industry in the nineteenth century.

THE MEETING
****

Elizabeth Maybrey sat before her dressing mirror on a cold autumn morning stirring at her reflection in the glass. The image that looked back at her was pleasing enough, although she would have preferred to have been fair rather than dark haired, as this was more acceptable these days. "Do you think I'm plain Mamma?" she said running her fingers through her hair. "That painting of you in the drawing room, the one with your Mother you seem to be about my age when it was painted, you look so beautiful in it I do wonder sometimes if I will ever be as beautiful as you."

"Nonsense child," replied her Mother, gently brushing her hair. "Your fair skin complements your dark hair and eyes. You are only fifteen Elizabeth and already you carry yourself very well, your Father and I love you just the way you are."

Elizabeth gave her Mother a hug, she loved her very much.

"Are you feeling better today Mamma? You don't look well lately what did doctor Redmond say when he called yesterday."

Charlotte Maybrey took Elizabeth's face between her hands. "You must not worry darling, the doctor suggested I get plenty of rest, I'm sure I will be feeling better soon. Come now, we must go down to breakfast, your Father will be waiting for us in the dinning room, he has a full day ahead of him, the mill won't run itself, hurry now be quick."

William Maybrey sat in the dinning room tapping his fingers angrily on the table. "For heaven's sake Mary where are they? They always seem to be late these mornings".

"They will be here any minute sir, "replied the maid nervously. The door opened and Charlotte entered with her daughter.

"I'm so sorry William it was entirely my fault, I quite forgot the time" said Charlotte looking quite flushed.

William grunted something and gestured to the maid to serve the breakfast. Kindly as he was to his family, William was typical of a nineteenth century land owner. A determined man, with a good business mind, who had inherited his property from his parents at the age of forty two. They had both died in a fire at the mill, five years earlier. William had a lot of his Fathers ways, determination being one of them. And in a few short years had rebuilt the mill, giving lots of work to the people of Bardsley. The work was hard for these people, starting at six in the morning until seven or even nine o'clock at night. The wages were very low, but at least in this mill there was always work available even for their children who were sometimes permitted to sleep in the afternoon. Things hadn't been going particularly well for William lately. A few of his workers had been holding secret meetings, trying to stir the workers up, to demand higher wages and better working conditions. He had found out by accident, needless to say he wasn't very pleased. He would go to the mill today and confront whoever it was causing all the trouble. These types of things had to be stopped before they got out of hand. William looked at the clock "Goodness look at the time! I must leave at once. "Mary! Mary!" Where is that girl? Why are servants never around when you need them"?

Mary opened the door, "Did you call sir? I'm sorry, I was just getting the tray to clear things away."

"Go quickly and tell Matthew to bring the carriage around to the main entrance, I'll be leaving at once."

"Yes sir right away". Mary shook her head as she walked down the hallway to the kitchen. Why? Oh Why? She thought is everyone always in a hurry in this household.

Charlotte gave a sigh of relief as she made her way to the kitchen, to talk to cook about the food menu for the day. She was glad William had left; sometimes he could be so tiresome. It was exhausting trying to keep this large house running smoothly, and almost impossible to find experienced staff these days, especially people who were used to working in houses such as these. The last one was enticed away by Mrs Fitzroy of Hollingwood Manor, not five miles away. The cheek of that woman, she never quite forgave her. Oh? Well, at least there was no gossip about this household like some she could mention

Elizabeth stood at the dinning room window looking out into the grounds that surrounded Berkeley Grange. Everything looked so beautiful at this time of year. The red and gold of the trees, and the crisp leaves under ones feet. How she loved this house, she felt safe here, although it had been a bit lonely being an only child. Her Mother had given birth to two other children before Elizabeth but unfortunately they had died in infancy. This was one reason why she felt so close to her Mother. She had been worried about her lately; she didn't seem at all well. Maybe this morning she would take a walk down to the river giving her time to rest.

Choosing a woollen cloak and hood from the hall cupboard she walked to the kitchen which was at the far end of the house. Her Mother stood in the pantry doorway with Ada the cook checking how many preserves they had for the winter.

"Mamma do you mind if I go for a walk, it's such a nice day?" asked Elizabeth.

"No, not at all dear, you go and take as long as you like."

"Will you promise to rest while I'm gone?"

Charlotte smiled to herself. "Of cause I will darling have a nice walk?"

Elizabeth walked out into the gravelled courtyard, she clutched her cloak tightly around her, it felt quite chilly. She decided to take a short cut through the vegetable garden. As she entered through the large wooden gateway, she saw Jo the gardener busy cleaning the soil off the winter vegetables, so he could take them to the kitchen. He looked up and acknowledged her.

"Good morning Miss Elizabeth."

"Good morning Jo, you won't mind if I take a short cut through your garden?"

"Not at all miss you go ahead, mind yourself the grounds uneven".

Leaving the garden through a small gate at the far end, she made her way down a steep pathway through some woods coming out into a clearing. From here she could see the whole town of Bardsley and beyond. She soon came to the river, the water was very high with all the rain they had had lately. It was rushing along as if in a hurry to get to the next county. She couldn't really believe that all this land would be hers one day. She wished she could share it with the whole world. And remembered what her Mother had said, that nobody really owned land, they were just caretakers looking after it for the next generation. Pulling her hood up she made her way along the river bank, she noticed someone on the other side of a large willow tree. Walking around the tree she could make out a boy, he was about seventeen, he had some kind of rod and he was fishing. As she stepped into his line of vision he turned, shouted something dropping his rod. He started backing away as if he was frightened of her.

"Please don't be scared," said Elizabeth. "Who are you and what are you doing here? You do know this is Berkeley Grange land?"

"Please miss my name is Michael O'Shea, my father is Jonathan O'Shea. We work at the mill for your father; I've seen you with him in the village. You won't tell him I was fishing here will you? If he found out I would lose my job."

"Why did you risk coming here to catch fish? Why couldn't you buy them in the market?"

"We are poor people Miss, a fish costs two pennies; we have young'uns at home to feed."

"Who's we? "Oh of cause you're Father. Do you have a Mother?"

"No miss she died two year back from consumption of the lungs."

"Do all your family work for us?"

"Yes bairns an all miss."

"I would appreciate it, if you could address me as Miss Maybrey instead of miss all the Time."

"Yes miss eh? Miss Maybrey."

"Why are you not at work today Michael?"

"It's Saturday today I get one Saturday off a month"

"Oh I see, you seem to have an accent are you Irish?"

"Yes were all Irish, my Father came to Manchester five years ago from the south of Ireland to find work, he's a weaver by trade. While he was in Manchester he heard they needed men in a mill near Bardsley, so he came along and your Father gave him a job."

"I'm sorry about your Mother Michael. How do you manage with the little ones? "

"We do ok; they can be a real handful sometimes". The oldest is sharna she's thirteen then there'S Luke ten, John eight, and the youngest is Hannah she's six, pa helps as much as he can. It's not easy but we manage."

"Are you in one of the tied cottages next to the mill? Asked Elizabeth

"Yes, number twenty four."

"Well Michael you had better get yourself home, your Father may need you. I promise I won't mention this to my Father."

"Your so kind miss, I won't fish here again honest" he said, walking away.

Elizabeth stopped him.

"Michael, I didn't say you couldn't fish here. If you come on your days off, make it between seven and nine in the evening. My Father will be dinning then, no one will see you. And if you come on a working day, you could come early before you start work. There won't be anyone around at that time."

"That would be great, thanks a lot! Is it ok if I take these fish home now?"

"Of cause you can, I hope you enjoy them. Good- bye Michael".

"Good-bye miss."

Elizabeth watched him disappear over a hill. He was a surprisingly handsome boy with fair curly hair. And under that dirty face the greenest eyes she had ever seen. Suddenly shivering with the cold, she thought she had better make her way back now, she hadn't meant to stay out this long. The thought of a nice hot drink made her quicken her steps. She soon came to the driveway leading up to the main entrance of the Manor. As she approached, she noticed her Father's carriage in the drive. What's he doing back so soon she thought? He's usually gone all day, better go in through the kitchen entrance he may have company.

Cook was baking cakes with the maid, it was so warm in there and the smell was delightful.

"Miss Elizabeth! Where have you been?" said Ada shaking her finger at her, you'll catch your death out there. Come and warm yourself by the fire. Mary, get a stool quickly."

Ada made her a hot drink as she warmed herself by the fire. Elizabeth asked her if she'd heard her Father come in.

"There was a rather loud noise about five minutes ago; I thought it was Matthew leaving by the main door. That man always seems to know when I'm baking."

After warming her hands and feet for awhile Elizabeth rose and walked to the door leading to the hallway.

"Thank you for the tea Ada. Did Mamma go for a rest?"

"Yes miss about a half hour ago. "

"I'll go and see if she's all right"

"Shall I put some tea in the morning room for your Mamma Miss Elizabeth?"

"That would be kind thank you Ada. "

Elizabeth heard voices as she walked down the hallway. The library door was slightly ajar, there seemed to be two men with her Father. They were pleading with him, saying the people of the town were very unhappy about working conditions at the mill. They were also telling him that they couldn't afford to buy coal to keep their families warm. Only last week one of the men's new born babies had died from the cold, also his own grandmother had succumbed to the cold aged sixty one. Her Father seemed angry. Didn't they know by now that people died when the winter was an exceptionally cold one? It had been happening as long as he could remember. One of the men started to raise his voice in a threatening manner. Her Father warned them that if they persisted in this way, he would dismiss them all and install the latest machinery to do their work for them, then where would they be. ! Also they should take note that soon this was going to happen anyway. Didn't they realise this was eighteen thirty five, things were happening very fast in the cotton industry. Technology was moving along and he was going to move with it. There was a long silence and fearing the door would open Elizabeth backed away quickly.

Reaching the stairs she climbed to the first landing just as her Mother appeared at the top of the stairs.

"Elizabeth! What on earth is going on down there? Whose voices can I hear?".

"Please don't upset yourself Mamma. It's just Father talking to some of his workers."

"Are you sure there's nothing wrong? Your Father never arrives home this time of day."

As they descended the stairs into the hallway, the library door was flung open and two men walked past them very agitated and red faced. They left by the main entrance slamming the door. Elizabeth's Father came out of the library almost bumping into Mary who had come from the kitchen carrying a tea tray.

"Watch were your going girl" he said glaring at her.

"I'm sorry sir I didn't see you. Shall I put the tea in the morning room?"

"I don't care where you put it, I didn't order it," Elizabeth stepped forward.

"I ordered the tea Father for Mamma. It's all right Mary; take it to the morning room we will be there shortly."

"Yes miss. Mary could feel that the atmosphere wasn't too good so she scurried away as quick as she could.

Charlotte turned to William. "William! Will you kindly explain what's been going on? What did those men want and why were they so angry."

"What happened here doesn't concern you Charlotte, It's just business matters."

"I don't agree William; anything to do with the mill should be discussed between both of us. If there is a problem I would like to know about it."

"Would you really, Well I'm sorry to have to say this Charlotte, but your duty is to keep this house running smoothly and to see to all our needs. I must ask you not to interfere in any business matters from now on. I will solve this problem by myself in my own time. Now if you don't mind I have an appointment to keep, I will be back this evening for dinner."

Elizabeth watched her Father leave, and turning to her Mother she noticed how pale she had gone. Taking her arm she guided her to the morning room sat her by the fire and gave her some tea. Sitting opposite her she remained silent until her Mother spoke.

"Elizabeth! Have you any idea what that was all about? Your Father has never spoken to me in that manner before. He has always in the past discussed everything appertaining to the mill."

"Well I can only tell you a little of what I heard" said Elizabeth, taking hold of her Mothers hands. "The two men seemed to be discontent about the conditions at the mill. Also people were dying because they could not afford coal," Charlotte interrupted her.

"Rubbish I've never heard of such a thing. They are obviously trying to hold your Father to ransom, to get more money out of him."

"But Mamma they seemed so genuine."

"I'm sure they did Elizabeth. If there is any truth in what those people were saying, I'm sure your Father will do the right thing." She rose from her chair. "Now enough of this, what are we to do today. I thought we would go into Bardsley to order some bolts of cloth to be made into drapes for the dinning room, the others are so old and faded. What colour do you suggest, plum maybe or rose damask."

Elizabeth was sure her Mother was trying to change the subject. Oh, well she would go along with it.

"I think it's a lovely idea Mamma let's have luncheon there too."

The coach made its way down the long drive through the main gates, then turning right onto the main road. The morning mist had cleared and a pale winter sun shone between the trees. Elizabeth mentioned to her Mother how bare everything looked coming up to winter.

"When the weather improves Mamma you will feel a lot better I'm sure".

Charlotte took Elizabeth's hand and squeezed it tight. "I'm quite sure I will dear". When the spring arrives we shall go away for a few weeks or more, how would you like that?"

"Will Father be able to go too?"

"I'm not quite sure if he will have the time but I will ask him."

As the coach pulled up in the main square they had almost forgotten it was Saturday, market day. The place was bustling with people, the weather hadn't stopped them putting up their stalls and trying to sell their goods. Elizabeth would have loved to wonder around the market but she knew her Mother wouldn't allow it. It wasn't their place to mix with the towns people.

As they stepped down from the coach a woman came over to them begging for money, she had a baby in her arms. Elizabeth noticed how ill she looked; before she could speak to her Matthew their coachman chased her away.

"Don't give them any money miss" he said waving his arms at her, "They will pester you forever".

"Matthew is right Elizabeth, once they take your money, they'll never leave you alone."

"But her baby may have been hungry Mamma."

Matthew laughed. "Most likely go on drink miss Elizabeth, don't waste your breath on them they wont thank you for it."

Elizabeth glanced back at the woman; Matthew hadn't seen what she had seen in the woman's eyes. The money was for her children she was sure of it."

They walked across the road to the drapers while Matthew stayed with the coach. It was a large establishment selling not only drapery, but material for ladies gowns, as well as a millenary and haberdashery section. All heads turned as they entered the shop, it was very busy. Elizabeth noticed somebody they knew at the far end of the shop. It was two of the Arlington family from Monkford Hall, Mrs Arlington and her daughter Emily; she waved to Emily who she liked very much. She was quite an excitable person but Elizabeth thought a lot of her because she had a heart of gold. She came over to them with a big grin on her face.

"Have you heard, there's going to be a charity ball at Hollingwood Manor? We've had an invitation already; Mamma and I are so excited, have you had one yet

Elizabeth?"

"No we haven't received an invitation, I'm not sure if we will be able to go, Mamma hasn't been too well lately."

"I'm sorry to hear that, it's going to be the event of the year. We came into town today to buy some of that beautiful organza to be made into gowns for Mamma and myself. I just love the pastel green, and I think Mamma favours the blue, I can't wait to see them finished."

"I'm sure they'll be very nice Emily. Will you excuse me I have to help Mamma choose some drapery for the dinning room?"

"Oh! Of cause, I'm sorry, please make an effort to come Elizabeth we haven't seen enough of you lately I miss you."

Elizabeth smiled at her "I will I promise."

Charlotte chose some deep pink damask material and was pleased to hear they would only take a week to be made up. They said their farewells to everyone, and left. It had started to rain heavily as they made their way back across the road to the white Swan Inn. A large thatched building built around fifteen forty. It had huge oak beams and big inglenook fireplaces, which always had enormous logs burning in them. The main room was set aside for the local gentry, serving the best ale and food available. The ordinary people of the town had their own entrance and bar; there was a lot of noise coming from there. On entering the publican rushed forward apologising for the noise. He was a very big man with a large red nose; Elizabeth couldn't take her eyes off it. She had to stop herself from laughing; it looked as if he had been drinking too much of his on ale.

"Welcome, Welcome, Mrs Maybrey. It's nice to see you again. It's been a long time, How are you? I hope your well."

"Yes quite well thank you landlord, we require somewhere quiet to have lunch."

"Of cause! Of cause ! I've just the place, please come this way," He led them to a back room which was small but cosy; there was a very old gentleman fast asleep in the corner.

They ordered some beef broth with bread and goat's cheese and some ginger ale, and then settled down to warm their hands and feet by the fire. After eating their meal they felt a lot better.

"We should do this more often Mamma," said Elizabeth brushing the crumbs off her gown.

"Yes I agree with you, although your Father wouldn't approve of us coming here, he'd think this place quite immoral. I don't want you mentioning it to him It's our little secret."

"I promise I won't say a word, it will be our secret. Mamma. What do you think of this charity ball at Hollingwood Manor? Emily is quite excited about it."

"Well you know what I feel about those people Elizabeth, that woman would annoy the good lord himself. Mrs Fitzroy thinks she is above everybody else. Her Father was a Presbyterian minister and her mother a seamstress, she just married well."

"Mamma, as you know I haven't ever been to a ball before, it sounds ever so nice, is there any chance we may be able to go?"

Charlotte looked at Elizabeth. "Oh dear, I'd quite forgot what a young lady you are now. I went to my first ball when I was a year younger than you I promise I'll think about it"

"That's all I ask Mamma, I wouldn't want anything new to wear, I just want to be there to hear the music and watch people dancing".

"I remember I was absolutely terrified at my first ball" said Charlotte. I was shaking so much I trod all over this boy's feet. I was upset because he avoided me all night. He was extremely handsome, I vowed I would never again attend a ball, but of cause I did. Three years later I met your Father at a garden party, he was so dashing and good looking. He could have had any young lady there but he picked me, we were married a year later."

"Oh how romantic Mamma, I hope it happens to me like that one day."

"I'm sure it will darling one day. Now let's be on our way it's getting late."

****

CHAPTER TWO

A VISIT TO THE MILL

****

Elizabeth awoke to the rain beating heavily on her window pane, she sighed, why! Oh why does it always seem to rain on Sundays? She sat up and shivered, it was freezing, putting on a robe she walked to the window. Her bedroom overlooked the rear of the house. Terraces led to a rose garden below, everything looked bare and wet. Maybe she would get washed and dressed and go and see if Ada had made any tea yet. There was a lovely warm fire in the dinning room and the table was already set, good old Ada we would be lost without her. Sitting by the fire she noticed a poetry book on the table her tutor had given her to study over the weekend. As he was about to come first thing in the morning she thought she had better make an effort, and read some of it before her Father and Mother appeared for breakfast. Sundays were not very relaxing as they had to attend church at eleven o'clock. Her Father insisted they all go every Sunday; it was their duty to be seen there, as it gave a good impression to the locals. Elizabeth sighed; As if those people cared if they attended or not. Preacher Goodbody put so much fear into the poor souls it's a wonder anyone came. She wasn't very impressed with Preachers or church procedures. All she seemed to hear was death and damnation. And if they so much as missed putting a penny on the church plate, their souls would burn in hell. The only thing they seemed to care about was squeezing as much money as they could out of people. Her Father paid money every year to sit with his family in the gallery together with the gentry of the parish, the people of the town sat below. Elizabeth thought she would dearly like to know where the money went too. As it surely wasn't spent on the poor people of the town.

Later they had a nice breakfast together, although her Father did go on a bit about the workers and the mill. Apparently he didn't find out who instigated the trouble, whoever it was didn't come forward when he confronted them. Things were back to normal now and production was proceeding well. Elizabeth noticed her Mother hadn't to much to say, she supposed by her silence it was the best way to keep the peace.

The outing to church was not as bad as Elizabeth expected, she enjoyed the drive very much. After the service they drove past the grave yard. There were lots of people standing around, some were crying. As they past by it seemed to Elizabeth as if everyone turned and stirred at them, she felt quite uneasy. She wondered if it had anything to do with those people who died.

After returning home the rest of the day was taken up with piano lessons. Her Mother was a very accomplished pianist who liked nothing better than to encourage other people to play. Elizabeth knew she would never be as good as her Mother, but she enjoyed it, and the pleasure she got after learning a piece of music was very satisfying.

Later on in the evening they sat by the fire reflecting on the day's events, and then a little later retired to bed.

The Berkeley household was woken on Monday morning by somebody banging the huge knocker on the front door. Ada shouted to Mary to answer it at once before it woke the devil himself. Mary struggled to slide the bolts back on the front door, standing there was a very wet young boy holding his horse with one hand and a letter in the other.

"Letter for Mr and Mrs Maybrey from Hollingwood Manor, can't stop? Be back tomorrow for the reply" Then disappeared into the rain. Muttering to herself Mary closed the door. "No manners those delivery boy's, don't know how they keep their jobs."

William opened the letter as they sat eating breakfast. It was indeed an invitation for all of them to attend a charity ball on the twenty first of November, in aid of the local hospital, donations to be made on the night. Much to Elizabeth's delight her Father agreed it would be a good idea to go.

"I hear there may be influential people there" said William looking pleased. "Business men who have an interest in the railways. It could be beneficial to us, I've been thinking for a while of transporting our goods by rail."

Charlotte dropped her tea cup onto her saucer with a clatter "William why can't you just go to the ball to enjoy yourself? Instead of thinking about business all the time."

"You of all people should know by now Charlotte that business is conducted at charity events all the time. This is how things are done these days."

"I shall never understand men, if I live to be a hundred. They strive all their lives to better themselves and when they accomplish this, they never relax to enjoy what they have."

"You must understand dear, that if I relaxed and took it easy as you suggest, within no time at all there would be somebody that much quicker than me to snatch away my business."

"Oh I suppose your right. But promise me you wont disappear all night as you did at the last event, we scarcely saw you all night."

"Well I'll try not to disappear as you put it, but I can't promise anything."

"I will be too busy inspecting everyone's gowns Mamma to worry where Father is" said Elizabeth looking excited. "I expect they'll all be dressed very handsomely don't you think?"

"Which brings me to the subject of attire" Charlotte said winking at Elizabeth. "William did I tell you we bumped into Mrs Arlington and her daughter on Saturday. They were at the drapers selecting material to be made into gowns for the charity ball."

"It wouldn't mean by any chance that you and Elizabeth need new ones too does it? You women have an art when it comes to getting what you want. As this is a special occasion you can have them, as long as you don't spend a fortune."

"Oh thank you Father" said Elizabeth throwing her arms around her Fathers neck and kissing him, "I'm so excited."

"Alright! Alright, he said grinning. "You women know exactly how to get around me."

"Can we go tomorrow to order them Mamma; it will be here before we know it."

"Perhaps not tomorrow Elizabeth, in a few days dear."

After breakfast everyone seemed to call at once. The doctor arrived together with Elizabeth's tutor Mr Samuel Robertson. Quite an elderly man, a retired school master and a good friend of the family who taught pupils privately. Mostly to keep active but above all because he loved teaching so much. Elizabeth adored him, he was always smiling and telling her funny jokes and his enthusiasm for life rubbed off on her. It was lonely in this big rambling house and she looked forward to him coming.

They both settled down in the library and spent a couple of hours discussing poetry, Elizabeth's favourite topic. Then at eleven o'clock they ordered some tea and biscuits and chatted for awhile. Elizabeth couldn't wait to tell him about the charity ball.

Samuel assured her she would be the handsomest lady there and that all the gentlemen would be buzzing around her like bee's round a honey pot. She assured him that she wasn't as sweet as he made out. He hadn't ever seen her in a temper.

"Did I ever tell you Elizabeth about a dinner I once attended; it would be about three years ago. There was a particular gentleman; I think his name was Thomas Stanford. He was a maths teacher poor chap couldn't see a thing. He had a very badly made wig on; it looked like a dead cat on his head. Anyway at dinner the host's little dog took great exception to it, leaped up, grabbed it and disappeared. I don't think they ever found it again."

Elizabeth was quite overcome with hysterical laughter. "Oh Samuel I don't know where you get these stories from, I'm sure you make them up as you go along."

"No I assure you they are quite true" he said grinning. "Well! Better carry on with some work. I think your Mamma will be wondering what all the noise is about."

They stopped to have lunch with Charlotte about twelve thirty, then studied till about three o'clock in the afternoon. Samuel had an appointment at three thirty, so Elizabeth said good bye to him and thanked him for a lovely day and she would see him tomorrow. After seeing him to his carriage she went looking for her Mother, she found her in the kitchen talking to Ada and Mary.

"How did your visit with the doctor go Mamma? Did he find you well?"

"Yes thank you dear. He said if I take it easy and don't do too much I should be all right soon. We have a bit of a problem Elizabeth. Mary tells me she has to go away for at least a month to her parent's home in Manchester, as her Mother is unwell. I'll have to find a replacement, as we won't be able to manage without a maid. Ada will need help, she cannot do everything. It's so hard to find people these days that are clean and honest."

"I'm sorry to have to do this to you Mrs Maybrey" Mary said looking upset.

"Good heavens Mary it's not your fault. You go and take care of your Mother, give her my regards and tell her I hope she'll be well soon. You can go first thing tomorrow morning."

Elizabeth woke the next day to the sound of somebody walking along the landing; she slipped out of bed and opened the door. It was Mary; she was creeping along the landing trying not to wake anyone.

"Are you alright Mary do you need any help" Elizabeth said yawning

"I'm sorry Miss Elizabeth did I wake you?"

"Oh! That's all right Mary. Do you want me to give you a hand with your bags?"

"No thank you I can manage really, I only have a small bag."

"Do you have anyone to take you to Manchester?"

"My brother is meeting me in Bardsley; I will be just fine thank you."

"Well good luck."

"Good-bye miss."

Elizabeth looked at the landing clock it said six thirty, no good going back to bed now she thought, might as well get dressed. The house was very silent, as she crept down the stairs. She made her way to the kitchen, Ada wasn't up yet, she poured herself a glass of milk from the larder and sat by the fire, it was still warm from the night before. She wondered why it seemed so quiet this morning, then she realised the rain had stopped. Walking to the door she peered out, it looked a nice day. The rain had freshened the air, to pass the time away before everyone got up; she decided to go for a walk.

It took about five minutes to reach the river; it was very high almost to the top of the bank. The branches of the old willow tree hung down into the water, they seemed to be dancing in the water. She walked along the bank for a few minutes enjoying the spectacle; suddenly she heard a voice behind her. It was Michael back again with his home made fishing rod over his shoulder, grinning from ear to ear.

"Good day miss Elizabeth hope you don't mind me coming to fish again. You did say it was ok, didn't you?"

"Good morning Michael. Yes I did say it would be all right, I don't know how you can possibly catch anything today though; I think all the fish have been swept away by the current."

"You could be right about that miss, but I have to try, if I don't catch anything today we don't eat tonight."

Elizabeth stirred at Michael. "Are you serious? You mean you go without food if you don't catch anything."

"That's right miss, Pa had to spend this week's money on some second hand shoes from the market for two of the bairns, them kids go through shoes like you wouldn't believe."

"Michael tell me something. The workers at the mill, are they so badly off? I've understood for a while now that people who work for us have it quite hard. But I didn't know you went without food or clothing."

"Well at the mill we do get some food during the day, around twelve o'clock. They give us water porridge with oat cake in it. They put onions in it to make it taste. It sounds awful I know, but it fills your belly and warms you up. Gets a bit tiresome eating the same things every day, but it helps Pa from having to feed us."

"Don't you have anything else besides that; don't you get meat and vegetable dishes?"

"Yes we do twice a week Wednesday and Sundays. I miss out on Sundays because

I'm off work, well at least in the afternoon. In the morning we have to clean our machines. The orphans at the apprentice house get the meat on Sundays."

"Are yes Mamma took me once, I remember a very disagreeable man arguing with Mamma. He didn't approve of me being there, said it was no place for me. Mamma reported it to Father but he said the man was right, I should not have been there."

"I know who you mean" Michael said pulling a face. "That would be Mr Scarsfield, he and his wife are in charge of the apprentice house, he has a bad reputation that one."

"How do you mean a bad reputation?" said Elizabeth looking bemused.

"There's talk that he beats them kids real good. That's all I'm going to say, ok miss."

"I understand Michael. Tell me, did your Father explain about the trouble at the mill the other day?"

"Oh sure, Pa said the men were really mad. There was a meeting in the yard behind the mill; they elected two men to go to the Grange to talk to your Father. I don't know what happened after that, I asked Pa but he said nothing had come of it."

"Can I ask you about the workers at the mill Michael, and how you are treated; you don't have to answer if you don't want to."

"Well I shouldn't be talking about this to you really miss. You promise you won't tell your Father."

"Of cause I wouldn't say anything to him; it would be between you and me. I know you don't know me to well, but you can trust me."

"How come you don't know anything about the mill? When your Father owns it, If it where my mill I'd want to know everything about it".

"Well your quite right of cause, I suppose I've had a very sheltered life. I have visited the mill on numerous occasions when I was younger. It was an adventure to me to see the machines spinning the cotton. I remember thinking once when I was about eight how lucky all the children were to be doing what they are doing. I didn't realise they were working for a living. Since then I've only been allowed to view everything from the office located high above the factory floor. Its only lately I've come to understand how other people are living."

"Me, Pa and the kids don't do to badly. It's the people who are sick and still have to work that I feel sorry for" Michael said shaking his head, If they don't work they don't eat."

"I can't imagine how it must feel to be so hungry, as I've always had plenty to eat" Elizabeth said looking sorry for him.

"Well we won't always be poor if I have anything to do with it, I will find a way to help my family, and we have our pride you know."

Elizabeth saw how embarrassed he looked, she realised she might have offended him. "Please forgive me if I've offended you, I didn't mean to imply I was any better than you."

"Oh that's ok really, I had better go now I'm late for work, I'll not catch anything here today."

"I hope I haven't kept you too late, talking to you. Michael, if I were to leave some food outside the kitchen door this evening would you accept it?"

"Well as long as it was only for the bairns's miss."

"That's what I meant, for the children, only for the children."

Michael smiled at her. "Thanks a lot, I'll be back about nine, you won't even know I've been I promise."

"Oh! Before I forget Michael, what's the name of your sister? The eldest one."

"It's Sharna miss. Why would you want to know that?

"I cannot tell you right now. Do you think you could come Thursday night after work?

"Yes I suppose so" he said looking puzzled. It will be late though after nine o'clock."

"That will be fine see you then." Elizabeth watched him go; she couldn't help feeling sorry for him. It must be quite a burden taking care of all those children with no Mother.

Breakfast was underway when she returned, it smelt really good. She washed her hands in the kitchen and made her way to the dinning room. Her Father and Mother where already seated.

"Are! There you are Elizabeth" her Mother said patting the seat next to her "Come and have your breakfast dear you look frozen."

"Good morning Father, good morning Mother. Sorry I'm late I walked along the river bank, its quite a sight, the river is really high with all the rain we've been having."

"Elizabeth, I'm not sure if I approve of you going down to the river at this time of year" said her Father. "It could be dangerous."

"Elizabeth's a very sensible girl William; she wouldn't put herself in any danger. It's good for her to take the air, and the exercise will do her good."

"Well! I suppose your right Charlotte, just be careful. Do you hear!

"Yes I'll be careful I promise. Father, I would like to ask you something? Now that I am coming up to my sixteenth birthday. Isn't it about time I started taking an interest in the mill. I know in the past you've never liked me visiting the mill, but I'm older now, and would very much like to take an interest in the business."

William looked at Charlotte. "Well! Well! Well, I had no idea you thought that way Elizabeth. Being a girl I thought you were only interested in dressing up and all that stuff ladies do"

"Good heavens William, give the girl credit for something." said Charlotte looking surprised. "One day the mill will be hers, she will have to acquaint herself with all aspects off running a mill."

William looked quite shocked, "Her husband will you mean, in a couple of years we will have to seriously think of finding a husband for her. Someone in the same business we are in. Come to think of it, a mill owner's son would fit the bill nicely."

"Really William! Elizabeth is not one of your bales of cotton. You just can't marry her off to anyone, even if he is the son of a mill owner. What ever happened to the idea of marrying for love? I don't remember you ever being interested in how wealthy I was when we first meet."

"Well that's because we where equals Charlotte, you weren't exactly poor were you. And anyway it's different with Elizabeth, she's very young and needs guidance."

"Stop please" said Elizabeth, "Anyone would think I was looking for a husband, which I am not! . It will be years yet before I even think about anything like that; I'm not even sixteen yet."

"Quite right" said Charlotte shaking her head. "Time will come soon enough for marrying; you have lots of time to think about that when you're older."

Elizabeth changed the subject quickly. "Mamma, I think I might have found you a suitable girl to replace Mary, she's hard working and honest." I hope this girl whoever she is wont let me down, thought! Elizabeth, crossing her fingers under the table.

"How did you find somebody so quick dear? I haven't even started to look yet"

"Oh, Mary mentioned it before she left. Shall I have her come to see you on Friday Mamma? I think she will make a good house maid."

"Why yes, that would be alright on Friday" Charlotte said looking pleased.

After breakfast Elizabeth had her usual music lesson with Charlotte. Then at ten o'clock her tutor Mr Robertson arrived with the delivery boy in tow.

"I found this young man outside; I think he wants a reply to an invitation delivered yesterday."

"Thank you Samuel" said Elizabeth. "Will you come to the library and warm yourself by the fire while I write out an acceptance card for the boy."

Elizabeth's tutor didn't stay long; he had to leave early that day, so the afternoon was free for her and her Mother to do whatever they pleased.

"Now young lady what would you like to do today" asked Charlotte.

"You have worked really hard at your studies, Samuel said you are an exceptional student, and he is very pleased with you, so today, you! can pick where we go."

"You did say anywhere Mamma? And you won't change your mind?"

"No dear I won't change my mind."

"Well I would like to go to the mill only this time I want to see everything, and not sit in the office like I usually do."

"But Elizabeth it's dirty and the noises from the machines are terrible, you have to shout at one another to make yourself heard. Can't we go to the swan again and have a nice lunch?"

"Mamma you promised you wouldn't change your mind remember."

"Oh all right, but I won't be showing you around, I'll get whoever is in charge to do it. Go tell Matthew to bring the carriage around; I just have to talk to Ada to tell her we won't be back for a while."

The mill was just a short distance from Berkeley Grange. A very grand red brick building, built around seventeen thirty, six storey's high, with a very high chimney at one end. It stood in a landscape of rolling hills just outside the town. Elizabeth's Father had automatically taken over the business after the awful fire five years ago.

As the mill came into view from the carriage window, it seemed so much bigger to Elizabeth than the last time she was here. They drove through the main gates and stopped at two very large wooden doors. Matthew jumped down from the carriage and pulled a large iron bell pull a few times until somebody answered. They made their way to the manager's office up lots of stone staircases; Elizabeth's Mother could hardly make it to the top.

"Why I let you talk me into this Elizabeth I shall never know" said her Mother out of breath. "I hate to think of what your Father is going to say when he finds out."

"I'm sorry you're out of breath Mamma you can rest now we are here."

As they entered the office a very large man in his late forties jumped up from his desk looking extremely startled, he had a bottle of some kind he was trying to hide in the drawer. Charlotte stepped forward and said.

"Are you the manager?"

"Why yes Mam, Smithfield's the name, George Smithfield."

"I don't remember you, Are you new here?"

"I've been here about a year Mam, I took over after the other man who died"

"Well, It's been a while since I was last here, do you know who I am"

"Why of cause Mam, your Mrs Maybrey, and I presume this is Miss Elizabeth. I had no idea you where coming this afternoon, Mr Maybrey never mentioned anything."

"The reason being that I didn't tell him we where coming. Do you have a problem with that?"

"Oh, no Mam! Of cause not. What can I do for you? Mr Maybrey is not here today he got a call to go to Manchester on business."

"Yes, he did mention something this morning about it" Charlotte gave a sigh of relief, Good he's not here she thought! "I would like you to give my daughter a complete tour of the factory. You're to take her where ever she wishes, do you understand! It should take quite a while; I'll be back with the carriage at four thirty. You don't mind if I call for you later do you Elizabeth?"

"No by all means Mamma you go ahead I'll see you later." Elizabeth saw her to the door.

"Right miss where would you like to start?" asked Mr Smithfield looking very uneasy

"I would like to see the entire operation from beginning to end. If that's all right."

"Yes of cause, please come this way, I must warn you in some parts of the factory the air is full of cotton fibre's you will have to cover your face."

"I'm sure if these good people who work here have to endure it every day of their lives, I will be able to stand it for a couple of hours Mr Smithfield."

They made their way down a lot of stairs and corridors to where the cotton bales were unloaded from the wagons, which brought them from the Liverpool docks. The raw bales were then weighed on huge scales, then graded and sent up to the mill.

Mr Smithfield explained to Elizabeth how the cotton was shipped from America or the West Indies by boat to the Liverpool docks then transported to the mill via Manchester. After a while they made their way to the carding room which prepared the cotton for spinning. Elizabeth stood in wonder at all the activity going on. There seemed to be children no more than ten years of age running around working on large machines.

"Mr Smithfield "Elizabeth asked. "How old are these children? They look so young to be working on what looks like dangerous machinery."

"Your quite right miss, all the machinery is dangerous if you don't know what you're doing. Some children are younger than they should be. But you must remember their parents need them to work to bring money into the household, two wages can't sustain them."

"How much does a man earn in a week then. Do you know?"

"Well I think the men get ten shillings a week and the women five shillings. The children get nine pence."

"That seems very little reward for working so many hours, I don't know how these little ones work so long, surely they don't do the hours the grown up's do?"

"No not the little ones, but the twelve year olds yes, they work just as hard."

"And what's the accident rate? I presume there would be accidents from time to time."

"Well, I really shouldn't be discussing this type of thing with you miss. It may upset you, why don't you mention it to your Father. He will tell you everything you wish to know."

"Why is it that every time I ask questions about what happens here at the mill, I'm always told it's not my place, or I'm too young? What is the secrecy about? Anything you say to me will not go any farther than these walls."

"There's no secrecy miss, it's well known that the accidents in some mills is high. We are quite lucky here we've only had one death this year."

"You mean people die doing this work? Your quite sure about this, you have seen this with your own eyes."

"Oh yes, I had to cut a girls hair off to release her from under the spinning mule, between the roller beam and the carriage. We couldn't save her."

"What was she doing under the machine" asked Elizabeth looking extremely shocked.

"She was what we call a scavenger. They have to crawl under the machines to brush out the cotton fibres that accumulate underneath. This type of thing happens when children get tired towards the end of the day. I believe the girl took her cap off, probably because of the heat. She must have got her hair caught in the machinery. It gets really hot in there, eighty to eighty five degree's sometimes; it wasn't a pretty site I can tell you. We nearly had a riot on our hands that day. It took us a while to get things under control. If it had been one of the towns children, things would have been a lot worse, but it was only one of the children from the apprentice house."

"Not so bad, how can you say such a thing. Just because she was an orphan doesn't mean she was any less a person than the towns people. On the contrary, we should have had more compassion because she had no family."

"I'm sorry miss; I didn't mean anything by it I'm sure. Your quite right of cause, you get hardened after so long in this business, it's not always that bad. There are a few people who lose fingers and such like, usually through lack of concentration. Times are hard at the moment, people are just thankful to have a job."

"I've seen quite enough in here" said Elizabeth, "Please take me to where they weave the cotton."

"Are you alright miss? You look awful pale; can I get you some water?"

"No Mr Smithfield I'm perfectly well carry on." Elizabeth didn't want to admit that she felt quite faint.

They ascended two more flights of stairs through a door into an enormously long room where the mule spinning was again in progress. These machines were nearly the full length of the room. Spindles of cotton spun round at enormous speed, the noise was deafening. Elizabeth put her hands over her ears and gestured to Mr Smithfield she'd seen enough. They carried on through the dyeing and weaving sections, coming out into the printing room, then made their way down a huge flight of steps to were the source of the power was that ran the mill. A wonderful large waterwheel which used the water from the river, that ran under part of the mill.

"How wonderful" said Elizabeth, "How does it work Mr Smithfield?"

"Well the water is fed over the top of the wheel making it turn, which in turn, rotates that shaft up there. It goes through the wall into the factory to power the machines, very clever don't you think."

"I'm quite taken aback, I had know idea any of this was here." Elizabeth said looking surprised.

"The waterwheel system has its drawbacks, when the water is low at certain times of the year we don't get the power we need which makes production drop. That's why your Father is introducing steam power into the factory. There is a great need for cotton here and abroad. As your Father says it makes sense to change over to the latest machines."

"Will this mean people will lose their jobs Mr Smithfield?"

"I suppose some jobs will go miss, we don't know yet how many. I think we had better make our way back now it's nearly four thirty."

"Yes I agree, thank you for showing me round it's been very interesting, shall we go."

****

CHAPTER THREE
THE CHARITY BALL
****

Elizabeth lay in her bed that night tossing and turning thinking over the days events. How blind and ignorant she was to life outside these walls. Her parents had kept her in this cocoon of safety, not subjecting her to the world outside. She'd had everything given to her from the time she had been born, but today her eyes had been opened a little. What she had experienced today looking into those little faces, was something she would never forget. Wiping tears from her eyes she vowed one day to put things right, which her family had not.

Michael stood under the big willow tree down by the river, sheltering out of the wind. It had gone nine thirty; maybe she'd forgotten he was coming. No! She'd remembered to leave the food by the kitchen door hadn't she, and this was Thursday night. Suddenly he heard his name being called.

"I'm here miss by the willow tree" he said waving his arms.

"Oh, there you are Michael, it's so dark I could hardly see you, I'm sorry I'm late I couldn't get away. I can only stay for a minute I will be missed. I brought you some cheese and a bit of bread it's all I could get."

"Thank you miss that was kind of you. What did you want to see me about?"

"I want you to tell Sharna to wait outside by the kitchen door tomorrow at ten o'clock; I may have a job for her. Our house maid has had to go away for a while and we need a replacement. It should pay more than she's getting now."

"I don't know how to thank you miss, she'll be so happy when I tell her. But I've just thought, isn't she to young to be a maid she's only thirteen "

All she has to do, is say she's fourteen no one will know. And before I forget, tell her she must be scrubbed clean and be dressed in clean clothes. This is most important, you'll remember that?"

"Yes, I'll remember thanks" He took her hand and looked into her eyes.

"This won't cause you any trouble will it."

She looked embarrassed at him touching her hand, but thought it a nice gesture. "No it will be fine really, I must go now or I'll be missed." She left him thinking what a kind soul he was.

Elizabeth heard her Mother calling her as she entered the hallway. She flung her cloak into the hall cupboard and shouted to her Mother she'd be there directly.

William stood with his back to the fire in the drawing room looking a little agitated. "Please sit down Elizabeth; I've called you and your Mamma here to discuss something.

"It's been drawn to my attention that you and your Mamma visited the mill yesterday without consulting me, can you explain?"

"Well I had no idea I'd need your permission Father as we had discussed the subject yesterday" William stopped her.

"We discussed it yes, but I don't remember giving anyone permission."

"And does this apply to your wife William? Asked Charlotte. "You seem to have a very short memory. Years ago we both agreed we would share everything, or have you forgotten."

"No I've not forgotten Charlotte, sharing certain things are all well and good, but the mill is another matter. It's up to the men of this family to run it as I'm sure you must understand."

"William we have no intention of interfering with the running of the mill. Good heavens we only went there because Elizabeth wanted to see how a mill was run."

"I understand that of cause my dear and maybe when she gets a bit older I'll explain everything she has to know."

Elizabeth sensed that it would be futile trying to ask her Father anything about the mill at this time, nobody would listen anyway. So she made some vague apology explaining she was very tired, and made a quick exit.

Friday morning after breakfast Elizabeth sat in the kitchen with Ada. She wanted to tell her about Sharna before she saw her and chased her away.

Ada wasn't to keen on hiring someone who hadn't worked as a maid before. But when Elizabeth explained that the children had no Mother, she changed her mind and said maybe it would be alright. Anyway she had no option they were short handed.

"At ten o'clock Elizabeth happened to look out of the kitchen window. And who did she see; only Sharna standing outside shivering in the cold, she opened the door.

"How long have you been standing there Sharna? You have no coat on, come inside quickly your freezing." Ada looked over at the little girl.

"Good lord child you don't look as if you've got a days work in you, you're as thin as a rake."

"I'm small for my age Mam, but I'm strong" Sharna said standing up straight to make herself look taller.

"How old are you girl" asked Ada shaking her head.

"I'm fourteen Mam."

"Oh well! No way of proving that I suppose, you'll have to do. Go with Miss Elizabeth and see the lady of the house, she'll want to see you."

In the hall Elizabeth whispered to Sharna, "Don't be afraid, I'll help you, let me do all the talking. I think Mamma's in the drawing room. Have you got that?" Sharna nodded. Charlotte looked up as they entered the room. "Mamma, this is Sharna she's come about the position as house maid."

Charlotte looked her up and down. "Come here child, how old are you? You look a bit too young to me."

Before she could answer Elizabeth spoke, "She's fourteen Mamma, she looks younger I know. She needs the position badly, as there is only one parent at home, her Father."

"Does the Father work for us?"

"Yes Mamma, if you agree to take her on, I'm willing to help Ada to train her. She seems very willing to learn."

"Oh very well, she'll have to do; I haven't the time to find anyone else. Will you find her a room in the servants quarters please Elizabeth. There's one next to Mary's room that's empty I think."

She took Sharna up the stairs along the first landing, through a door at the far end which led to the servant's quarters at the back of the house.

"You must not come the way I brought you Sharna, there's a staircase from the kitchen leading to your room, and you must use that one."

"I will thank you miss"

Elizabeth soon found the room and unlocked the door. The room was small with a slopping roof at one end. The furniture consisted of, a bed, one wardrobe and a wash stand. Sharna looked around.

"Am I the only one sleeping here miss?"

"Of cause, why do you ask that?"

"I've never had a room all to myself before, I always slept with my brothers and sister."

"Well you have now" Elizabeth said smiling at her. "You have it all to yourself so enjoy it. You should be able to start working here tomorrow. Be here by seven o'clock; bring anything you want, within reason of cause. You'll find bedding and working clothes in that cupboard, Ada will explain everything to you tomorrow. Do you have any questions now?"

"Mr Smithfield will want to know why I'm not at the mill today and tomorrow. What shall I do?"

"That's all right Sharna; I will send a note tomorrow explaining everything."

"You've been so good to me miss Elizabeth. My pa told me to tell you he would light a candle especially for you on Sunday, and may god bless you."

"That is really kind of your Father dear, tell him thank you from me. Now I'll see you out, we'll go down the back stairs to the kitchen."

Elizabeth couldn't keep her mind on her lessons after Sharna left; she made some excuse to Mr Robertson, and told him if he didn't mind, could he come back on

Monday. He said it would be quite all right and left.

After lunch Charlotte suggested they go into Bardsley to select some material for their gowns, and get a fitting at the dress makers. Elizabeth liked the idea immensely and rushed up the stairs to change. This was going to be the most exciting thing that had ever happened to her. Her very first ball.

As they drove up the main street of Bardsley, there didn't seem to be many people around, except a few beggars crouching in doorways out of the cold. They made their way to the drapers, it wasn't at all busy, and so they had plenty of time to pick what material they wanted. Charlotte picked blue taffeta with white accessories and Elizabeth chose a pale grey satin with pink roses for the waist and some for her hair. Everything was very expensive, but Charlotte new that William would want them to get the very best. She wanted him to be proud of them on this special occasion. Next stop was the dressmakers; the woman took all the details of what they had in mind for the gowns. She said it was short notice, and, there was so much work to do on them, but as they were such distinguished customers she would start them right away. Charlotte seemed tired after spending an hour with the dressmaker, so Elizabeth suggested they go home to get some refreshment.

The weekend came and went quietly, not like Monday which started with Elizabeth having to teach Sharna how to lay a table for breakfast lunch and dinner. And to Elizabeth's amazement she only made a couple of mistakes. After a while she realised, to her great relief that it would only take a couple of days to teach her the basic things, and she would be able to leave her to work on her own.

The rest of the week was spent down by the river talking to Michael, before and after he had to go to work. It meant she had to rise early but she didn't mind. She enjoyed his company; he taught her how to fish, and where the best places were to catch them. Elizabeth couldn't get over the excitement she felt on catching her first fish, she wanted to put it back in the river, but remembered why Michael was there. It was probably his supper, so she said nothing. He asked how Sharna was doing and if she was behaving herself, she told him they were very pleased with her, she was learning very quickly, and she was a hard worker. Michael explained she was the smartest in the family, and knew she would do well whatever she did. The little ones missed her a lot but they would get over it, anyway they could spend part of Sundays with her which wasn't too bad. Elizabeth told him all about the charity ball that was to take place on the twenty first of the month and how excited she was. How she'd had a special dress made for the occasion.

"Do you have to go far to this place miss Elizabeth?" asked Michael as he stuffed the fish into his bag.

"Oh no, it's about five miles west of here, on the road between Oldham and Manchester. The house is called Hollingwood Manor; I have been a couple of times with my parents, its really beautiful almost twice as big as Berkeley Grange."

"It sounds really grand, if I ever get to go to one of those balls will you dance with me?" he said his face going quite red.

Elizabeth laughed, "Of cause I'll dance with you Michael and that's a promise I'd also like to stay here a bit longer but I have to go, I'll see you soon."

"Did you enjoy fishing?" he said flinging the bag over his shoulder, if you like we could do it again sometime."

"I would love to fish again Michael, thank you for the lesson. I must go now I'll see you soon."

The day arrived of the charity ball; there was great excitement in the Maybrey household. Matthew drove into Bardsley very early to collect the gowns and bring them back, so they could be checked over, to see if there were any last minute alterations to be done.

Elizabeth waited patiently for his return. Sharna didn't understand what all the fuss was about, but soon realised why. When the huge cardboard boxes were opened, every one gasped in amazement at the gowns.

"Oh, Mamma! Mamma ! How beautiful" said Elizabeth, holding her gown in front of her? Charlotte took hers from the box.

"Well, I must say she's done wonderful work, I'm very pleased with them."

"Come Mamma lets try them on, "Sharna! Help me take the boxes upstairs. Sharna! Did you here me." The little girl stood stirring at the box, with her mouth wide open.

"She's quite overcome," said Elizabeth laughing. "It's all right Sharna. Would you like to help us when we try the gowns on?" She nodded taking one end of the box.

The gowns fitted beautifully, Elizabeth couldn't wait till five o'clock when it would be time to get ready. Matthew was bringing the carriage around at seven, that would give them lots of time.

Elizabeth stood before a long mirror in Charlotte's room looking at herself, her Mother had put her dark hair up in curls, with a pink rose behind her ear and seed peals around her neck. The grey satin was perfect with the pink. She put her arms around her Mother with tears in her eyes.

"Mamma, I don't know how to tell you, how happy I am. Do I look nice?"

"Do you look nice, Elizabeth! Why you look beautiful, you quite take my breath away. I don't know where you got the idea you were plain."

"Well! Emily Arlington once told me the only really beautiful women in this world were fair haired ones."

"I don't suppose it had anything to do with Emily being fair would it Charlotte said laughing.

"It may well have been Mamma. Look here, here I am talking about myself, what about you. Wait till Father see's you in that gown he'll be so proud."

"Why thank you Elizabeth I do hope so."

They had quite forgotten Sharna who was sitting on the floor, she looked very tired. Charlotte pulled her up. "You poor child your falling asleep, I quite forgot you sitting down there, Elizabeth and I can manage now. You have been a good help to us today, go and ask Ada to give you some supper, and then go to bed." The thought of food made the little girl make for the door.

Soon after eight o'clock the gates of Hollingwood Manor came into view. Poplar trees stood proud along each side of a long drive leading to up to a very large Elizabethan Mansion. Huge bay windows shone with the light of hundreds of candles in every room, designed especially to welcome guests on their arrival. There must have been a dozen carriages lined up along the drive, waiting to disembark their passengers.

After a while they pulled up at the main entrance, a boy helped them down from the carriage. He wore a red jacket and white silk pantaloons with matching shoes. Charlotte whispered to Elizabeth, "Trust the Fitzroy's to show off like this, you would think royalty was coming."

"Well I think its wonderful Mamma; I can't wait to get inside."

William led them up the steps through the main doors into a large hallway with oak panelled walls and a beautiful carved wooden staircase. Someone took their invitations and cloaks, and pointed to the end of the hallway. They could hear the sound of music, it sounded like a waltz being played. William took Charlotte's arm and entered a very large room; an orchestra was playing at the far end. Huge candelabras hung from the ceiling and the room was filled with people dancing to the music. Everywhere seemed to be swirling colours of blue, lilac, pinks and white from the ladies gowns. Elizabeth was speechless.

"Mamma, I had no idea it would be this wonderful" she said taking her Mothers hand. "I'm so nervous, promise you won't leave me for a while?"

Charlotte was about to answer her when a very large lady came towards them. It was the hostess Mrs Arnold Fitzroy, overly dressed with to much rouge on her cheeks. Elizabeth thought she reminded her, of a doll she had received for her birthday when she was little.

"Mr and Mrs Maybrey! I'm so pleased you were able to come tonight, particularly you Charlotte, its been ages since we have had the pleasure of your company, I must show you all the changes we've made to the Manor since you were here last."

"I must apologise for not replying to your invitations Mrs Fitzroy" said Charlotte. "Business you know."

"Really Charlotte? Call me Esther please, we have known each other for ages."

"I'm sorry! Esther."

"My goodness! Don't tell me this is little Elizabeth, why she's all grown up. I don't know if you'll find any eligible young men tonight dear, they all seem to be some what taken with my daughter Louisa. She's quite exhausted with all the attention."

"I assure you Esther, Elizabeth is here tonight only as an observer, being her first ball, we want to introduce her into the local society you understand."

"Of cause of cause! I understand, go ahead now and enjoy yourselves.

William seated them comfortably near the orchestra and gave them some warm punch. "Well Elizabeth! What do you think of everything so far," her Mother said gazing round the room. You seem to be quite relaxed now, are you enjoying it.?"

"Oh Mamma! I love it, the music, and the people. Where do they all come from? I see a few people I know, but most of the faces are new to me."

"They come from far and wide to these charity balls dear. It's supposed to be all about collecting for the poor, but mostly it's about business, keeping abreast of everything that's going on in the world. The women, well, their here to support their husbands, and to get the latest gossip of cause."

"Surely it's not all about business; everyone seems to be enjoying themselves."

"Of cause not, people enjoy it immensely, but remember, this is not the real world. Some people lose sight of what's really important in life, money isn't everything. Will you remember that?"

"Yes Mamma I'll remember."

A young man came over and asked Elizabeth for a dance. With her heart pounding she accepted. She was so glad now for the dancing lessons she had taken some time ago. The young man introduced himself as Edward Hyde a lawyer, of Hyde and Sons from Manchester. Elizabeth told him who she was. He said he knew her Father; he sometimes visited his Fathers law practice in Manchester.

"How come I haven't met you before Elizabeth? Don't you attend many charity events?"

"No I don't attend too many, I've been to busy of late," She found herself going quite red, and hoped he hadn't noticed. She wasn't going to admit it was her first ball. After a while the music stopped, he thanked her for the dance and took her back to her seat.

Her Mamma was dancing with her Father, how grand they looked, her Mamma looked so happy, she wished this night would never end. As she glanced around the room she noticed Emily waving frantically on the other side of the ballroom. She was sitting with her parents. Leaving her seat she made her way over to them.

"Good evening Mr and Mrs Arlington, Emily! I hope your well?"

"Elizabeth I can't believe its you, you look amazing" Emily said touching her hair. Haven't you noticed everyone stirring at you? You've got Mrs Fitzroy's daughter Louisa quite green with envy."

"No surely not, you do exaggerate Emily."

"I'm telling you it's true, you've already danced with the boy she's been after for ages."

"This is silly, really! I don't know any of these people; I'm here just to have a good time'

"I'm so glad you said that Elizabeth, now you can talk to me all night then, it will be like old times. Come I'll show you where the food is, I'm starving. They have the most wonderful selection of fruit from abroad, some I've never seen before."

After sampling some of the delicious food the two girls sat in a corner of the room chatting about what they had been up to these last few months. Elizabeth explained she had been busy with her studies, and how her Mamma hadn't been very well.

"You really should get out more Elizabeth you'll become melancholy in that big rambling Manor. You need younger people to talk to."

Elizabeth told her about Michael and how she had been spending her time down by the river.

"You'll have to be careful talking to people like that, Elizabeth. How do you know he's not trying to get to know you so he can rob you? He could easily find out when you would be away, and enter the Manor."

"No! Michael would never do such a thing; he's a hard working boy who's trying to do the best for his family."

"How can you acquaint yourself with such people Elizabeth? My Mamma would be incensed if I so much as mentioned having spoken to any of them."

"But Emily they are people like you and I, with feelings and aspirations for the future, just like anyone else."

"Well I suppose if you look at it that way, but you must admit Elizabeth they don't have the same capacity for leaning as we do. Well that's what Mamma says."

"No Emily I think your wrong, the reason they can't achieve anything in life is for one reason only, they were born poor. They haven't had the opportunities we have had."

"Why I never thought of it like that before, I suppose you could be right. You have always been a kind soul Elizabeth, but you must be careful though, if your Father were to get to know you've been talking to one of his workers you would be in trouble and the boy would lose his job."

Oh dear, she could be right, thought Elizabeth, I'd better stop seeing him, I don't want to get him into trouble.

The night past quicker than she wanted it too. There were so many young men asking her for dances she was quite worn out. By eleven thirty Charlotte was ready to go so she asked Elizabeth would she mind if they left.

"I could dance all night Mamma it's been so wonderful but I can see you're tired, I'll just say my good-byes to Emily and her family and meet you at the door."

Emily was sorry she had to go, "Now don't forget to call on us at any time Elizabeth, will you promise?"

"Yes I promise, I have a birthday coming soon, we will do something together how's that."

"You mean it! Great I'll hold you to that," she said giving Elizabeth a hug "Good-bye dear Elizabeth see you soon."

Mrs Fitzroy came over to them as they collected their cloaks and bonnets.

"Leaving so soon Charlotte cant you stay a little longer?"

"No I'm afraid not William has to be up early tomorrow, he has an appointment in Manchester."

"Well thank you for coming and for the generous contribution to the hospital, safe journey goodnight."

Eight thirty the next morning Sharna tapped on Elizabeth's bedroom door.

"Miss Elizabeth! Are you awake, can I come in?"

Elizabeth woke with a start, "Sharna what is it, is anything wrong?"

"Oh no miss. Your Father asked me to tell you and your Mamma to come to the dinning room right away. He wants to talk to you both before he leaves for Manchester."

"I must have slept in with all the excitement last night, tell Father I'll be there directly."

"Yes miss."

William was sitting in the dinning room drinking his morning tea.

"Thank you for coming so promptly" he said gesturing them to sit opposite him. There's something I have to discuss with you before I make a big decision which will affect all of us. As you know Charlotte I've been seriously thinking about expanding the business, and exporting abroad. At the moment water power is sufficient for our needs, but if we want to expand we have to go to steam. This involves buying the necessary machinery which is very expensive not to mention the installation. I wish there was another way to do this but there isn't. do we have to expand Father, are we not making enough money?" asked Elizabeth"

"Yes of cause we are Elizabeth, at the moment. There is a chance a depression is on the way. Quite soon we will start to lose orders because other mills can deliver sooner than we can. And the reason being they have the latest machines."

"Do you mean that if we don't install these machines, in time the business could be in trouble?" asked Charlotte.

"I'm afraid so. We either go with progress, or we get left behind, it's as simple as that."

"But surely if there's a depression on the way don't we have to save money instead of spending it?"

"No dear it's just the opposite, if we can't get the orders from this country we have to go and get them somewhere else. And to do that we have to go with steam power."

"Well I think you've already made up you mind William, other wise why would you be going to Manchester today?"

"That's not all together true Charlotte; I do value your opinion. What do you think about the idea?"

"I presume you have thought about this very carefully, and you have considered that it's not just our livelihood that's at stake; it's all those people at the mill as well. They have a lot more to lose than we have."

"Yes I've considered every aspect of it. If I don't do this, they may lose their jobs anyway."

"Well William you had better install your machines and hope they bring good luck and prosperity to us all."

"I'm so glad you've understood what this means to us Charlotte," said William, smiling broadly, "You won't regret it I promise."

Elizabeth sensed that what had just happened was rather serious, and hoped that the decision her Father had made was the right one for everyone concerned.

After seeing her Father out and wishing him luck and a safe journey, Elizabeth went to her room to get washed and dressed. She knew her Mother had retired to bed for a couple of hours, so she had plenty of time to consider what to do with her time today. Charlotte had asked Samuel, not to come today as they would be tired after attending the ball the night before. She told him to have a well deserved rest, and they would see him soon. Elizabeth made her way down the stairs to have breakfast;

Sharna was busy sweeping the stairs.

"Good morning Sharna. Have you settled in alright? If you need anything let me know."

"Thank you miss I'm fine, I've just put some fresh tea in the dinning room, can I get you anything else?"

"No you can get on with your work, if I need anything I'll get it myself. Don't go near Mamma's room she's having a rest."

"I won't miss I promise."

Elizabeth smiled to herself, this little girl was trying so hard to please, she'll be worn out if she tries to do too much. Maybe today would be a good time to try to get another girl to help out.

It was such a nice day Elizabeth decided to go around to the stables which were situated just behind the rose gardens. Her Family had two horses, one called Major her Fathers horse, and the other a mare called Ebony so called because she was black. Her Father and Mother had given it to her on her birthday two years ago. She loved her very much because she was so gentle. She would be missing her; it was ages since she'd been to see her. As she entered the stables she called out to john the stable boy.

"John are you there? I wish to take Ebony out for a ride?"

"I hear you miss, I'll be with you right away, just getting some feed to put in the stalls. You'll have to be careful riding her, she hasn't been out for a while, could get a bit frisky. She's stamping her feet already, she knows you're here."

"That's all right John I can handle her. Saddle her up I should be back in about an hour." The air was cold on her face, but felt so good as she trotted round the back of the stables, and down the lane. She headed for Hawks Peak a wild area high above the town, Elizabeth could see for miles around, it was perfect for riding. Ebony was keen to finely stretch her legs, so Elizabeth gave her, her head; they galloped a good mile, both enjoying each others company. Later she sat on a huge rock taking in the scenery, while Ebony enjoyed munching on the grass. She wondered if those people at the ball last night ever did this, somehow she couldn't picture them galloping across a field in the middle of winter. Life wasn't just about dressing up and going to balls and such like, she was sorry for them, they were missing a lot. She gazed down into the valley; the mill and the Apprentice House where very clear from here. What if she was to call at the Apprentice house? She wondered what her Father would say if he found out. Did she really care, if he wants me to take over the mill one day he shouldn't be surprised if I take an interest she thought? Mounting Ebony she rode the rest of the way over Hawks Peak down into the valley, and followed the road past the mill. The Apprentice House was half a mile down a narrow lane. She tied Ebony to a post and walked through the gate, the path led past a vegetable garden which looked very bare except for a few rotting cabbages. The house was a lime washed building three storeys high, older than the mill. It had once been the main house on the land before her family had acquired it.

Elizabeth walked up to the main door and knocked on it, there was no answer so she lifted a large iron ring and banged it down. That should get their attention, she heard footsteps coming down the hallway, the door opened revealing a some what large man of scruffy appearance with what seemed to be food stains on his clothing which had apparently been there for some time.

"Well what do you want?" he said eyeing her up and down.

"Are you Mr Scarsfield caretaker of this establishment?" Elizabeth presumed it was him, but she wanted to make sure.

"Yes, that's me, and what's it to you, if you have any business it's the mill you want, now be off with you."

"How dare you talk to me in that manner sir? Don't you recognise who I am; I'm Elizabeth Maybrey the daughter of your employer. I hope you don't greet everyone in that manner because if you do, you will not be in this position for long."

The man stirred at her with his mouth wide open, he stammered some kind of apology trying to button his clothing.

"Well are you going to let me in or not?" said Elizabeth waving her hand.

"If I'd known you were coming I'd have!"

Elizabeth finished his words for him. "Cleaned up! You mean, well this way it's a nice surprise," she said sarcastically. He led her to a back room, she presumed was some kind of sitting room, there was a woman sitting in front of a roaring fire with her feet up. Elizabeth's first impression of her was that she was no better than the man.

"Look who's here my dear, its Miss Maybrey herself come to visit us." The woman jumped up trying to smooth her untidy hair.

"This is my dear wife Winifred miss. If there's anything we can do for you, you only have to ask. Isn't that right Winifred," Scarsfield said nodding at his wife

"Well the first thing you can do is to show me round the house, Elizabeth said. "Are there any children here at the moment?"

"Not really miss, their all at work, there's a couple sick upstairs, but I'm sure you don't want to be bothered with them. I can take you to the school room it'll be more interesting for you."

"Mr Scarsfield, I have not ridden all this way to be entertained, I am here to check if the children are being looked after properly. After all it is your place to see that their well cared for, is it not!"

"Yes! Yes! Of cause miss, I can assure you my wife and I do a good job here looking after all these children. It's not easy you know, sometimes their so hard to handle. But they know their place; any trouble makers are soon stopped."

"And how pray? Do you do that" Elizabeth said, looking at the woman who seemed to be almost cowering in the corner.

"If they cause any trouble they have their money stopped."

"But I thought orphans didn't get paid any money?"

"No they don't, only if they do overtime, then they get paid."

Elizabeth didn't want to spend much time talking to this man; she had taken an instant dislike to him so she changed the subject.

"Well we had better start on the ground floor, the kitchen I think, and then the school room. The kitchen was quite large; it had a stone floor which had obviously never been cleaned for months. A long wooden table stood in the centre of the room with three large cooking pots on it. Elizabeth peered into one; it looked like some kind of porridge from the day before.

"Is this what you're feeding the children on? She said feeling a little nauseous."

"That's what's left over from their breakfast," Scarsfield said grabbing the lid and slamming it on to the pot. "Anything left over we mix oat cakes in it, then it does for their lunch, it's quite nutritious."

"Don't you ever clean this place it's filthy? Elizabeth said running her fingers over the table. "I've never seen such a mess. Its no wonder you have sick children here."

"Well you did catch us at an inconvenient time," Scarsfield said putting some dirty bowls into the sink.

"We were about to clean the place when you knocked on the door."

"You had better show me the school room," she said walking to the door. "I hope it's better than this for your sake."

There where the usual things in the school room, rows of desks with slates on them. A large blackboard stood at one end. The only light they had were candles which stood on shelves around the room, there didn't seem to be many books around.

"When do the children get their schooling Mr Scarsfield," asked Elizabeth.

"I take them at night if there's time, and a local school master takes them on Sunday afternoon's after church. They also have to wash their own clothes; we have them do other things like making candles from animal fat. And the girls make their own pinnies among other things."

"Can they read and write, you don't seem to have many books for them"

"Oh yes miss they read real well, the boys do better than the girls because the girls have more chores to do, but they do alright."

"Well I've seen enough here, you can show me the bedrooms and the attics now please." Turning into the hallway they climbed a narrow wooden staircase at the other end of the house. Mr Scarsfield explained that there was nobody in the boy's room at the moment as they were all at work.

"I'll take you straight up to the next floor were the girls sleep." he said puffing and panting his great body trying to negotiate the steep stairs. They entered a long room with a window at both ends. Wooden straw filled cots ran along both walls, there was nothing on the wooden floor. The fire place was empty, and the room seemed very bare.

"Its freezing in here, is there no form of heating Mr Scarsfield?"

"Heating costs money, we only get so much money every year to run this place, we put them two to a bed, they keep each other warm. We've never had a complaint, not even from the Select Vestry Committee, they inspect once a year."

"Who are these people I've never heard of them? Asked Elizabeth.

"Their a special Committee set up to investigate the state of affairs at the local workhouses. They send someone round once a year to check our orphans, as they come to us from there."

"I notice you and your wife don't go without heating in your living quarters?"

"Well we are here all day; the children are at work most of the day."

"Well that may be so sir, but there is nothing to stop you lighting a couple of fires for them at night in the winter time." Scarsfield didn't answer he just shrugged his shoulders.

"Mr Scarsfield I'd like you to go now and wait for me down stairs if you please, I'll be down directly as soon as I've finished here."

"It's best if you don't speak to the children miss, they need their rest, being sick an all.

"I'll decide what's best and what isn't" Elizabeth said opening the door for him to go.

"Right then whatever you say miss, I'll be down stairs then," he said, shutting the door.

Elizabeth walked down the room, and as she got to the bottom she noticed eyes peering over the blankets at her from a bed in the corner.

"Hello, I don't wish to frighten you, my names is Elizabeth"

What's your name?" A little girl sat up and just stirred at her not saying anything.

"Isn't there supposed to be two of you in bed sick?" The little girl pointed under the blankets.

"Oh, the other one is hiding from me I see! " Elizabeth sat on the bottom of the bed. "You mustn't be afraid; I'm just here to see how you are, and if I can help you. Would you like to tell me what your names are and how long you've been here?"

The girl pulled the other person from under the blankets; she was a couple of years younger, their ages seemed to be about twelve and eight.

"I'm Sarah miss, and this is my younger sister Amy, we've been here for one year, our parents died, and there was no other relations to take us in. So they put us in the workhouse, then after a while they brought us here to work in the mill."

"Do you like working in the mill? Asked Elizabeth feeling tears coming into her eyes.

"Its alright I suppose, we get a bit more food here than in the workhouse, and we can work in the garden in the summer. We both like gardening we used to do it at home with ma, when she was alive. Elizabeth noticed tears in the girl's eyes.

"I'm sorry you lost your parents it must have been awful for you both. I know this isn't the ideal place for you, but at least you are together. I can't help noticing you both have really bad coughs, how long have you had them?"

We've had them a long time, ma said, we had weak chests, she used to rub pig fat on them it smelt awful but it helped."

"Haven't you seen a doctor?

"Mr Scarsfield said it costs too much money to have a doctor call." Elizabeth jumped up from the bed. "That's ridiculous; Doctor Redmond wouldn't charge anything to look after orphans." Elizabeth walked over to the window; she looked out over the open fields thinking! What's been going on in this place, I haven't heard one positive thing since I arrived. And all this is going on in the name of Maybrey; she was determined to get to the bottom of it. She knew these children would not tell her anything on what was going on here, they would be too scared. She reassured them that somehow she would get a doctor to have a look at them the next day.

"Have you had any food today?" Elizabeth said looking around. "I don't see anything for you to drink. "

"No miss, nothing, it's alright, our friend brings us something at twelve o'clock when she comes for lunch."

"You should have had something, even if it was only a drink, I'll see what I can do, now try to get some rest, good-bye."

"Good -bye miss, and thank you."

There was another set of stairs leading to the attics, Elizabeth decided to have a look, and they ran the full length of the house. The attics were used for storing dry goods like oats and barley. There didn't seem much there except a few boxes of apples from the summer which were partly mouldy. She turned and went down the stairs to the sitting room to talk to the Scarsfields. They looked decidedly nervous.

"I hope everything's to your satisfaction miss," Scarsfield said rubbing his hands.

"It certainly is not, those children are really ill up there, and you haven't even given them a drink today. After I've left, you're to give them something, do you hear! And why haven't they seen a doctor yet?"

"Doctors cost money; we only get so much to run this place a year."

"Yes, yes, as you keep saying Mr Scarsfield, but the first priority must be the children's health do you not agree?"

"Well yes I suppose so."

"There's no supposing about it, that's how it should be, I'm leaving now, I will send a doctor tomorrow morning. And you can be sure Mr Scarsfield that I will be back soon to check on how these poor children are being treated. Good day to you sir."

****

CHAPTER FOUR
THE BIRTHDAY DINNER
****

There was great excitement in Bardsley as huge wagons entered the town with what appeared to be a very large boiler of some kind, and other wagons containing machinery and a lot of pipe. People stood on both sides of the road, most of them were from the mill. They had gone to work as usual that morning but when they arrived, they were told to go home and come back the next day. Mr Smithfield the manager had assured them that none of them would lose any money. This seemed to satisfy most of them but there was a few who were suspicious about what was going on. The people were scared of anything that might change their lives for the worse. Michael stood with his family wondering like all the others what was going on.

"Pa where are they taking all this machinery? Do you know?"

"It's for the mill son, that there, is a boiler that produces steam; they say it's more efficient than the water wheel. Nobody at the mill expected this to happen so soon, Maybrey the mill owner threatened it might happen. I only hope our jobs are safe, anyway we will soon find out."

Michael thought of Elizabeth, he wondered if she could tell him anything, she hadn't been down to the river for a few days. Maybe she was sick or maybe she hadn't even thought of him, he missed her very much. Dare not mention it to pa; he would only ban him from going anywhere near the river.

"What are we going to do today pa if there's no work. Shall I go fishing and catch something for supper."

"No boy! If there's no work we'll have to find some. We'll go up to the mill and see if they need any men. They must need extra hands to install all that machinery. Take the bairns to Mrs Cross; she's a good woman she'll look after them today. I'll wait for you at the mill."

They weren't the only ones trying to find work when they arrived. There must have been thirty men with the same idea. Mr Smithfield was there with William Maybrey, who was trying to quieten everyone down. Mr Smithfield had a paper in his hand.

"Right men," he said waving it around. "Here's what we want, we need only men that have had experience with any kind of machinery other than cotton looms. Also someone who's had experience pipe fitting. If you have, step forward, by the way, if you haven't I assure you we will know. "

"A few men came forward including Michaels Father. Michael pulled his Fathers coat whispering, "Pa you've never done them things."

"I have son, way before you were born," His Father yelled over to Mr Smithfield. "Got a boy here works real well with me, ok!" Smithfield looked at Mr Maybrey who nodded saying it was alright.

"Right, bring the boy along, all you men line up and I'll tell you were to go."

Charlotte and Elizabeth waited patiently for William to turn up for dinner that night, but he didn't arrive. Sometime later a messenger arrived with a note saying he would not be back till the next morning, they would be working all night to install the new boiler.

"Well you and I can have a nice relaxing evening Elizabeth," said Charlotte, "We'll just have each others company, it will make a nice change what do you think?"

"That's a lovely idea Mamma; I'll go and tell Sharna to get a couple more logs for the fire." Settling themselves down in front of the fire they both gazed sleepily at the logs in the grate, flames lapped around them, and the sound of cracking was very soothing. Elizabeth thought of the children in the Apprentice House they wouldn't be warm tonight, trying to dismiss it from her mind she closed her eyes and found herself drifting off to sleep. It wasn't long before she started to dream and it wasn't a very pleasant one. She dreamt she was in a large empty house, and every time she took a few steps she could hear someone behind her, but when she turned around there was no one there. Suddenly there was the sound of children crying coming from one of the rooms. As she opened the door the sounds stopped, there was nobody in there only a doll on the floor its head was cracked open. She came too with a start, her Mother was shaking her.

"Elizabeth wake up dear! You're having a dream."

"Oh, I'm sorry Mamma." Elizabeth said sitting up quickly. "I must have fallen asleep."

"It's not like you to have disturbing dreams dear, there's nothing upsetting you is there?" Elizabeth knew this was the perfect time to bring up the subject of the orphans at the Apprentice House. It wouldn't do any harm to mention it.

"Mamma, what do you know about the orphans at the Apprentice House?"

"Well not much dear. The children come to us from the workhouse, and work here until they are eighteen. It takes the burden off those institutions, from having to feed them, and the children get a roof over their heads in exchange for working at the mill."

"Mamma while I was out riding yesterday, I called at the Apprentice House and spoke to the couple in charge of the place, a Mr and Mrs Scarsfield. A very unpleasant pair who's hygiene has much to be desired. There were sick children there, who were not being looked after properly, and the place was freezing."

"Really Elizabeth I wish you wouldn't interfere with things that don't concern you. If your Father were to find out, you would be in a lot of trouble."

"But Mamma don't you care how your workers are treated. There is a rumour going on that these people are abusing the children."

"Rubbish Elizabeth, I don't know were you got the information from, I assure you your Father would not allow anything like that to happen to those children. As far as I know, he visits there regularly to keep an eye on everything."

"Well of cause everything may seem alright to Father when he calls there. If those people know he's about to visit, they will make sure everything's clean and tidy."

"Well I don't know dear, you know your Father hates us bringing up the subject of the mill. I'll tell you what, if he brings the subject up again I'll mention it, how's that."

Elizabeth looked at her Mother. Poor Mamma, she really doesn't have much of a say what happens in her own home, or anywhere else for that matter, she changed the subject

"Father will be very tired when he gets home tomorrow Mamma. It looks as if he's going ahead with all these changes to the mill. Aren't you surprised how quickly all this has happened?"

"I can see you don't know your Father very well dear. All that business about how he values my opinion, on whether we should go ahead with the changes. He's had this planned for months; he was going ahead with it no matter what I thought."

"And you never said anything. Why Mamma?"

"One thing you'll learn as you get older Elizabeth is that woman's wants are disregarded in the world today. It's always the men who have the last say."

"Well I hope if I ever get married my husband will take into consideration my feelings and hopes for the future. After all we both make commitments to one another."

"True of cause, Charlotte said smiling at her. "Unfortunately the man only has to say, I agree to keep her in sickness and in health till death us do part. Nothing about sharing important decisions together."

"Mamma you paint such a bleak picture of marriage, is it really that bad?"

"I'm sorry my love, I didn't mean it to sound glum. Of cause it's not bad, we have a very privileged life here, we want for nothing. Unlike those poor orphans you mentioned." "It seems as if life depends on what family someone is born into Mamma, whether they will have a decent life or not, it doesn't seem right some how."

"No of cause it doesn't seem right, I expect it will change some day, I hope so. But in the mean time this is how it is I'm afraid." Elizabeth was about to say something when there was a knock on the door. She shouted. "Come in."

"Its Sharna, Mam, cook told me to ask you, if there's nothing else tonight is it alright if we lock up and go to bed ?"

"Oh! Good heavens it's late," Charlotte said jumping up. "Tell cook I'm sorry for keeping her up so late. And yes she can lock up. "Thank you Sharna goodnight."

"Goodnight Mam."

"You go to bed Mamma, you really should rest more you are quite pale. I'll see to everything here."

"You're such a help to me Elizabeth," Charlotte said kissing her on the cheek, thank you goodnight."

The next morning Mr Robertson the tutor arrived about ten o'clock, just before William made an appearance looking very tired. He was in no mood to answer any questions, stating he must rest a few hours. He'd let them know all the news later, then left.

Elizabeth called Sharna to bring some fresh tea to the library. Mr Robertson was busy sorting through some papers. He looked up as she entered the room.

"How's my favourite pupil today" he said grinning at her, "Ready for some work?"

"You know I'm always ready to learn from you Samuel, you make learning fun."

"Well I won't be with you much longer Elizabeth. I've made up my mind that there's not much more I can teach you. You're very accomplished in all your subjects, so I've decided I must take my leave. I've enjoyed my time here very much, more than you will ever know. I've considered you, not only a friend but almost like a daughter. I want to wish you every happiness for the future, and if ever you need any help or someone to talk to, I'll always be here for you."

"Samuel I had no idea I was at the end of my studies. You gave me no impression that this was the end. Elizabeth put her arms around him and kissed him on the cheek. "You've been a good friend to me all these years Samuel I will miss you dreadfully. But you don't get away that easily, I'm celebrating my sixteenth birthday in two weeks time and I want you here, you will come?"

"I'll be here I promise, I would never forget your birthday, I was in this very house the day you were born. The happiness you brought with you was something none of us will ever forget."

"Thank you dear Samuel, that's such a nice thing to say. What are you going to do with your life now?"

"Well! I thought it was about time I retired."

"Samuel, you always say you're going to retire but you never do."

"Yes, but I mean it this time, I've been thinking for quite a while now about writing a book. I can keep my mind active, and at the same time rest when I want to."

"I think it's a wonderful idea, what is the book going to be about?"

"Oh just teaching in general, all the things I've learned over the years, it might encourage somebody to take up the teaching profession, you never know."

"That's just like you, Samuel always thinking of other people," How she loved this dear old man she would truly miss him. "Oh! By the way Samuel, do you know the teacher who teaches the orphans at the Apprentice House on Sunday afternoons. ?

"Yes that would be Mr Woodgate he teaches at the church school, a nice chap. doesn't get paid at all for giving his time to teach the orphans. He was orphaned himself once, a long time ago. A local family took him in and gave him a home; I think he's paying back the community for helping him. Oh! While I'm on the subject Elizabeth I meet Doctor Redmond in town, told me to let you know, he got your note. And to say he had called at the Apprentice House to see the sick children. Apparently the younger child is very bad, and has been taken to the local hospital, that's all I know."

"I'm sorry to hear that, I'll talk to him tomorrow he's coming to see Mamma."

"How is your Mamma lately dear? Every time I ask her how she is she always says she's feeling fine, but is she telling me the truth."

"I fear she's keeping back how ill she really is Samuel. She has a weak chest, and this weather is not helping any."

"Doctor Redmond told me there had been some deaths in the town. He said some can be explained, but there are a couple who have died, who have symptoms he hasn't seen before. He said he was off to Manchester tomorrow to discuss the matter with some doctor friends of his."

"Didn't he have any idea what it could be?" said Elizabeth looking puzzled.

"No I'm afraid not. Better not say anything to your Mamma it might worry her."

"No I won't say a word; she's worried enough about all the alterations to the mill. I suppose you have heard about it?"

"Yes the news is all over town, seems your Father is taking a big risk doing what he's doing at this time."

"How do you mean, risk Samuel? Is there something we should know about?"

"No, No, I'm sure things will turn out just fine for your Father. It's just a rumour going round that there's a recession on the way. We hear things like this every so often it never comes to anything."

"Well I'm sure your right Samuel we won't start worrying just yet. Now how about you and I sitting by that nice warm fire and having some tea… We can discuss that poetry book you left last week; it's the nicest I've ever read."

Two hours later Samuel said his good-byes to everyone, and gave Elizabeth the poetry book as a farewell gift, and left.

Charlotte was busy putting up the new drapes in the dinning room with Matthew that had arrived that morning. Elizabeth helped as much as she could and eventually they managed to put them up. And to every ones delight they looked very grand indeed.

"I must say they look very nice, don't they Elizabeth?" Charlotte said standing back to admire them. Your Father may even notice the change."

"I doubt it Mamma, he never seems to be aware of anything we do to the house."

"I suppose your right dear, he should be coming down soon, I'll go and talk to Ada about what were going to have for dinner tonight."

The discussion over dinner was all about the mill. Elizabeth was getting sick of hearing about it. When she'd eaten she decided to go for a walk, it was very late but she needed some air. It was cold but dry, she breathed deeply, it was good to get away from the house for awhile. She hadn't gone two hundred yards when she heard her name being called. She couldn't see anyone, and then as she passed a large oak tree Michael stepped out in front of her.

"Good heavens Michael you scared me half to death. What are you doing here? Your to close to the house someone will see you."

"I'm sorry Miss Elizabeth I just had to see you. I've waited down by the river for day's now and when you didn't come, I feared you were sick, or maybe your Father had found out about us."

"No Michael nobody knows about us, I've been getting worried someone might see us though. I don't want you to lose your job. I would never forgive myself."

"Oh is that all it is," he said beaming all over his face. "I thought maybe you were getting fed up with my company, seeing as I'm just a worker from the mill."

"I don't know why you should put yourself down like that Michael. I talk to you because your good company, as well as being kind and honest. So don't let me hear you saying things like that again. Do you hear?"

"I won't I promise miss. We can still be friend then, you'll come down to the river tomorrow?"

"I'll tell you what we'll do Michael, instead of meeting here; I'll meet you on Sunday afternoon on Hawks Peak. Do you know it?"

"Yes I know it, just above the mill, that large hill."

"That's the one; I'll be on my horse you can't miss me."

"You have a horse? That's great; I used to ride back in Ireland. We had to sell our horse to raise money to come here. I miss that old horse it was like losing a friend."

"I know what you mean; I would be devastated if I lost mine. I'll let you have a ride on Sunday; it will make you feel as if your back home."

"Do you mean it," Michael said his face going quite red. "Thanks a lot, I'll have to go now I promised Pa I wouldn't be long, one of the bairns are sick he needs my help."

"I'm sorry to hear that, can I do anything for you Michael?"

"No thanks miss there's nothing you can do; it's probably just a cold."

"All right I'll see you on Sunday good-bye Michael." She watched him disappear over the hill then made her way back to the Manor.

The following day Elizabeth had lots of time on her hands. There was no studying to do so she spent the day planning her birthday dinner with Ada. To Elizabeth the preparation was just as exciting as the day itself. Sharna got so excited they had to calm her down.

"Good heavens child" Ada said, "Anyone would think you'd never had a birthday."

"My Ma used to remember my birthday cook. I got a cake once it had cream on the top; I never ate it all day."

"Why ever not?" said Elizabeth

"Because once I'd eaten it, it would be gone forever."

"Ada and Elizabeth looked at one another and burst out laughing. "Oh Sharna, what a funny girl you are," Elizabeth said giving her a hug. "When is your birthday dear? Do you know?"

"Yes I know miss, it's the eighth day of December. I remember because it's the same day we sailed to come to England."

"Why that's two days before mine Sharna. We will have to make you a little birthday cake all to yourself. Would you like that?"

"Oh miss, do you really mean it. Will it have cream on the top?"

"I think you mean icing, Sharna, yes lots of icing. And you get to eat it all to yourself."

"Thank you miss. I promise to work really hard this week, and help cook as much as I can."

"Well start with the silver my girl" Ada said pointing to the table. "I want to see my face in them, jump to it."

Elizabeth promised Ada as soon as she could, she would find her another girl to help her in the kitchen. This pleased Ada no end, and before Elizabeth left, she was heard humming happily to herself.

Doctor Redmond arrived late in the afternoon looking very tired. Elizabeth gave him a cup of tea before taking him to see her Mother.

"How is that little girl from the Apprentice House doctor "asked Elizabeth "The one you took to hospital."

"Yes, I'm afraid its not good news. She died about three thirty this morning from pneumonia. She was diagnosed to late." Elizabeth was taken aback, her heart sank.

"Oh, no? That poor little girl. That man should be locked up and the key thrown away," she said feeling so angry. The doctor looked puzzled.

"What are you talking about Elizabeth, What man.?"

"That Mr Scarsfield, he didn't help those children, and he must have known how sick they were. And especially that wife of his. She of all people should have known better."

"I agree the conditions aren't good over there, but without proof I'm afraid we can do nothing."

"Doctor, will you promise me that you will visit the children more often. I can't explain why just yet, I have a bad feeling about the whole thing."

"Well of cause I will Elizabeth if you think its best, I can't think why you want this. But I'll do as you ask."

"Thank you doctor, I appreciate it, I'll take you to see Mamma now, she's upstairs lying down,"

After a while the doctor left saying he'd done all he could for Charlotte. To keep on with the ointment and it had to be applied to the chest twice a day. Elizabeth thanked him and saw him out to his carriage, and watched it disappear down the drive. The weather was exceptionally cold; with an eerie mist that hung over the gardens making it difficult to see more than a few yards. She shivered, not with the cold but with a bad feeling that swept over her, ignoring it she went back into the house to see how Ada and Sharna were doing. How Ada had managed without help in the kitchen she would never know. Tomorrow she would do her best to find someone.

The next day Elizabeth sat at her piano turning the pages over and over not being able to decide what to play. Finely settling on a piece of music, she played quietly so she wouldn't disturb anyone Her mind wasn't on her playing, she felt uneasy about a few things that had happened, over the last week or so. Her life up to this point seemed so superficial. Was she going to do as her Mother before her had done? Being the respected lady of the Manor, who only mixed with her own kind. She didn't want to follow in her Mothers footsteps never having a say in her own home. She loved her parents very much, and wouldn't want to hurt them in any way. But whatever happened she was determined to be a person in her own right, and stand up for the things she thought were right. The first thing I have to do she said to herself is to get a scullery maid for Ada, that would take the pressure off her, and she knew just the person for the job. Jumping up she went to the hall cupboard and put her bonnet, cape, and boots on. She left a message for her Mother saying she was taking the carriage and wouldn't be more than an hour.

Matthew wasn't very pleased at having to harness the horse to the carriage, complaining the fog was too thick to go anywhere. A sharp word from Elizabeth did the trick and soon they were on their way. She instructed him to go to the mill and he was to wait for her, saying she wouldn't be very long.

As they past through the gates of the mill one could hardly see the main entrance. The doors weren't locked thank goodness, so she made her way up three flights of stairs to the office. She knocked on the door, nobody answered so she went in, Mr Smithfield the manager was not there, she decided to wait. It wasn't long before she heard him coming up the stairs; he seemed startled as he came into the room.

"Why miss Elizabeth. What are you doing out on a bitterly cold day like this, is there anything I can do for you?"

"Good day Mr Smithfield, I must apologise for disturbing you, I know you must be very busy. I wanted to ask you about the orphans who reside at the Apprentice House. Are you familiar with any of them?"

"Why yes I have dealings with Mr Scarsfield all the time, we discuss where the children are best put to work. And which child is best for what job, that kind of thing."

"Then I suppose you know all about the child that's just died"

"Yes of cause, sad business that, pneumonia wasn't it?"

"That's right. What was the girl's last name? Asked Elizabeth. I know her first name was Amy."

"Its Price, Amy Price, I believe she has a sister there too."

"Yes its her I have come about, she will be very upset losing her sister like that. And it just so happens we need a scullery maid at Berkeley Grange. So I have decided to take her with me now."

"But I can't release the girl just like that, your Father has to authorise it, and he's far to busy to ask at the moment."

"That's exactly why I'm not going to bother him with it. And anyway he would only say yes to it. She's only one of the orphans, nobody will miss her and besides Mamma is ill and needs somebody right away."

"Well if you take full responsibility I suppose it will be all right. I'm sorry to hear Mrs Maybrey is not feeling her best. I'll go and get the girl right away, I won't be long."

Elizabeth gave a sigh of relief. Well that went better than I thought it would, she said to herself. Better get her out of here as quick as I can, in case Father makes an appearance.

Mr Smithfield was back five minutes later with the girl, who looked very frightened and as white as a sheet.

"Thank you Mr Smithfield for your help, I will certainly tell my Father how helpful you have been. I think I'd better get going before the weather gets any worse. Oh! By the way, if Mr Scarsfield causes any trouble, tell him to come and see me."

"Of cause miss I'll do that good-bye."

Elizabeth hurried the child down the stairs and into the carriage, and covered her with her cloak. It was surprising to Elizabeth that Sarah didn't ask where she was going or why she'd been taken from the mill. The little girl just stirred out of the carriage window not saying a word. Elizabeth took her hand and reassured her that everything was going to be fine and she was going to look after her. There was no response from the child only her little hand tightening its grip. Matthew was told to pull up round the back of the Manor outside the kitchen door. As they walked in Ada was making bread and nearly dropped the tins she was putting in the oven.

"Good lord above, what do we have here then, miss Elizabeth. Who have you got in tow this time?"

"Ada, this is Sarah your new scullery maid. I want you to give her all the attention you can. She's scared and confused and needs our help. Will you do that for me?"

"You poor wee mite" Ada said putting her arms around her. "You come with me, we'll give you a nice bath and get you something to eat. "I'll see to her miss, you go to the dinning room, dinner is in half an hour."

Charlotte was in the library sitting by the fire reading a book; Elizabeth kissed her on the cheek and asked her how she was.

"Fine dear, just a little headache. I've been waiting for you to come back. Is everything all right?"

"Everything's just fine Mamma, I've been to get a scullery maid for Ada. I don't want you to worry where I got her. She's a good girl who is going to settle in just fine so no questions, all right?"

"You're a good daughter to me Elizabeth; I promise I won't say a word."

Michael stumbled over the icy ground his heart pounding in his chest. He had been woken by his Father shaking him, telling him to run for the doctor as quick as he could, as his brother john was very ill. He prayed hard as he tried to keep his footing, he hoped the doctor was at home, he'd heard he was going to Manchester. Finely he reached the doctors house and banged on the door. It seemed like ages before the doctor opened the door. He shouted, "Who's there."

"It's me doctor Redmond, Michael O'Shea."

"Michael what's the matter boy, is John worse,"

"Yes doctor, Pa said to tell you to come quick, he's real sick,"

"Of cause Michael, just let me get some clothes on, and I'll be with you right away." As they entered the cottage Michael's Father was sitting with his head in his hands. He looked up and shook his head. "I think it's too late! too late! He just went so limp." Michael put his arms around his Father to comfort him, as the doctor ran up the stairs. A few minutes later the doctor came down, they knew by his expression that it was bad news. He didn't seem to be able to get the words out.

"I'm very sorry Jonathan there was nothing I could do. Will you please sit down I want to tell you something." They both sat down at the table hardly hearing what the doctor was saying. "I think both of you should know what we are dealing with here. I've tried to keep this quiet, but there are so many people getting sick that this has to be made public.

Your son John died from Typhus, a very nasty illness caused we think by bad living conditions. If you are healthy you may survive it, but those who are old or have a history of illness, it's those people who are most at risk. You and I know that John was not a strong child. The only advice I can give you is after we put your boy to rest, I want you to burn all the mattresses in the house, and to clean the place from top to bottom. We are all in for a very hard time, I fear. Tomorrow I will go to see Preacher Goodbody; I'll make arrangements for the funeral. You do realise he will have to be buried within the next two days."

"Why is that doctor? Michael said wiping the tears from his eyes.

"It's just a precaution Michael in case other people are at risk. I'm sorry for your lose Jonathan; I'm afraid there is nothing more I can do here now. I'll be around tomorrow morning to let you know the arrangements. You two better try to get some rest, there's nothing you can do for him now." Jonathan opened the door for him.

"Thank you doctor for your kindness, I will heed what you said, and thank you again." After he had gone they both held one another in their grief, then after awhile Jonathan made Michael go to bed.

"I will sit with your brother tonight son, this is one night he won't be alone."

Sunday afternoon Elizabeth waited for Michael at Hawks Peak. The sun was shining but there was no warmth from it. It had snowed over night leaving an inch of snow on the ground which sparkled like tiny diamonds. She looked down at the town, it looked like a picture postcard, Michael was nowhere to be seen. Hurry up Michael she thought! I have to be back home in an hour. Then she spotted him just below her, as he came closer she knew something was wrong. He wasn't his usual happy self, dismounting Ebony she tied him to a tree and walked towards him.

"I'm sorry I'm late miss I've been helping pa to clean the house, Doctor Redmond's orders, its taken two days."

"What do you mean Doctor Redmond's orders? Is there something wrong Michael? You look so upset" She sat him down on a rock; he had tears streaming down his face.

"We lost my brother John, he died last Thursday, the burial was yesterday."

"Oh Michael I'm so sorry," Elizabeth said putting her arms around him. "I remember you saying that one of the children wasn't feeling at all well. But I had no idea it was so serious. What did he die of?"

"The doctor said it was typhus, wasn't strong enough to fight it, he's always been a sickly kid."

"Do you know if any other people have it? Doctor Redmond never mentioned it to me the last time I spoke to him."

"He said there had been some, but I don't know how many. He did say the people of the town had to be told. There's a meeting in the church hall tomorrow night, pa and myself are going to see if we can help. There may be some way of stopping it spreading before it gets out of control." Elizabeth took out a handkerchief and wiped the tears from his face.

"I'm sorry this has happened to your family Michael, I wish there was something I could do."

"You've helped me more than you know miss, just being here. I've never met anyone like you before. You're the only thing that's clean and beautiful in my life, even if our friendship can't last."

"What makes you think it won't last." she said looking surprised.

"Because you live in another world than me, sooner or later we will be found out. An Irish immigrant is the last person in the world you should be talking to. That's what they'll say."

"I don't care what they say Michael, you're my friend and I can make friends with anyone I like. Anyway nobody comes here, this land belongs to my Father, which means it will be mine one day, so I can have as many friends as I like here. Now enough of being glum, come on I'll introduce you to Ebony she's getting restless. You can ride behind me till she gets used to you."

It wasn't long before Michael was riding on his own, he seemed to relax and for the time being forgot all his troubles. Elizabeth was amazed how he handled her horse, so gently, yet firm, she had never seen anybody with the skill he had, and she had been around horses all her life. Later they both sat looking out over the fields not seeming to feel the cold. Elizabeth had brought some bread and cheese which they both ate hungrily.

"Where did you learn to handle horses like that? She said to him. "They seem to like you."

"All my family have owned horses as far back as I can remember. My uncle in Ireland buys and sells them. Some he sells for local races and such like, I wish you could see them Elizabeth their so beautiful."

"You really have a feeling for them, don't you Michael?"

"Oh yes, I worked at a stables for two years before we came to England, it was the happiest time of my life. We used to exercise the horses every morning on the beach; it was such a good feeling."

"Well maybe one day you'll have horses of your own, Mamma says if you wish for something hard enough it may come true one day."

"No it won't ever happen for me, things like that only happen in fairy tales."

"Where's the fighting spirit you used to have Michael? Remember. You used to say you were going to better yourself one day. What's happened to change that?"

"Don't take any notice of me miss; I'm probably feeling sorry for myself losing John like that, it's been a really bad week."

"Of cause you must be feeling down at the moment," she said ruffling his hair. It's an awful thing to happen to anyone. Does Sharna know what's happened yet?"

"No, pa thought it was best if we tell her when she comes this afternoon. She was in a bad way when ma died; he thought it best to keep it from her till it was all over."

"Well I'm afraid I'll have to go," Elizabeth said jumping up, "I've stayed to long, Mamma will be getting worried. Will you be all right getting back home?"

"Yes it takes ten minutes that's all, thanks for the ride miss. Will you come again next week," he said helping her on to her horse.

"I'll be here next Sunday same time, goodbye Michael."

"Goodbye Elizabeth, Oh! You don't mind if I call you Elizabeth do you," he asked smiling at her.

"I wish you would," she said giving him a broad smile. "If I don't see you during the week I'll see you next Sunday. "

Elizabeth took Ebony back to the stables and walked back to the Manor. It will be good to get a warm, she thought!. Her Mamma was in the kitchen talking to Ada."

"Elizabeth, where have you been? You always seem to be disappearing these days," her Mother said looking for an explanation.

"I'm sorry Mamma I didn't realise I had been out so long."

"Your Father came home this afternoon ranting and raving, something about losing two people from the mill. They apparently died of something awful, do you know anything about it dear."

"I can't say I do Mamma, I'll just take my things off and I'll be back to help you."

Elizabeth's birthday came around quicker than anyone expected, but with a lot more hands to help around the place, everything went smoothly. The dinning table looked lovely, with the best china and silverware. Elizabeth made a beautiful centre piece of autumn foliage from the garden and the last of the summer grapes from Jo's greenhouse.

She took one last look around. Yes, that will do nicely; I do hope I've laid enough places. I'd better go and get dressed they'll be here in an hour. She made her way upstairs to find her Mother, she was getting dressed.

"Can I come in Mamma; I'm not disturbing you am I."

"No dear come in I'm nearly ready. Thank you for helping with your birthday dinner Elizabeth, its me that should be doing it for you."

"No you must not think that Mamma, I enjoyed doing it really."

"Well I'm sure you've done everything beautifully. Will you come here I want to give you something," Charlotte went to her dressing table drawer and took out a beautifully carved wooden box; she opened it and gave it to Elizabeth. The inside was lined with red velvet, and inside was the most beautiful necklace she had ever seen. It was gold with tiny diamonds and droplets of green jade. Elizabeth gasped!

"Mamma I cant except this. Isn't this the necklace Father gave you on your wedding day?"

"Yes dear, I want you to have it now, it was made for a young lady, and it's not to my taste now. Off you go now and select a gown to compliment it, go! And Elizabeth, happy birthday darling." Elizabeth gave her Mother a big squeeze.

"Thank you Mamma, thank you, it's so beautiful I can't wait to try it on."

Seven o'clock came and the carriages soon began to arrive. William greeted his quests looking very smart indeed. He had taken the opportunity of inviting a few business men, which Charlotte wasn't very pleased about. She whispered to him. "I thought this was supposed to be a birthday dinner for Elizabeth not a business meeting," he ignored the remark and kept shaking hands. Elizabeth was delighted when Emily arrived with her Father and Mother. And to her surprise Emily's brother who looked as if he wanted to be anywhere but there.

"I must apologise for my brother," Emily said quietly, "He just hates these family get togethers. He's not like me, I'm all for a free meal, and a good gossip."

"Really Emily you are a one" Elizabeth said giggling, "life would be very dull without you," She felt her Father take her arm. "Elizabeth I want to introduce you to a good friend of mine, Mr Hyde and his son Edward, they have a law practice in Manchester."

She looked at the son and recognised him as the person she had danced with at the Hollingwood charity ball.

"Good evening Elizabeth," he said holding out his hand. "I hope you remember me? I danced with you at the last charity event."

"Why yes I remember, how are you Edward. Thank you for coming out on such a terrible night as this."

"It's my pleasure I assure you, I hope I won't embarrass you if I say you are even more beautiful than the last time we meet."

"Why thank you Edward that's a very nice compliment," she tried not to laugh, poor Edward he sounded as if he had been coached to say every word. "Would you and your Father like to give little Sharna your things, and go to the dinning room. Help yourself to a warm punch while I see to the rest of the guests."

The only people that were late arriving where the Fitzroy's. As Charlotte said on many occasions they where always late so they could make a grand entrance, and Mrs Fitzroy certainly did just that, making sure everybody in the house heard what she had to say.

"Charlotte, how marvellous of you to invite us to your birthday dinner, I'm so looking forward to seeing who you have invited. Do you have anyone interesting! Where's the birthday girl, Are! There you are Elizabeth, how old are you dear, sixteen isn't it. Your Mamma was already engaged at your age, isn't that right Charlotte?"

Elizabeth interrupted her Mother. "Well things have moved on a bit from all those years ago Mrs Fitzroy. I think some women are realising that they have a choice in these matters. They don't necessarily have to be forced into marriage. Don't you agree Mamma?" Charlotte looked at Mrs Fitzroy, who's mouth was wide open, to shocked to reply. Trying to make a joke out of it Charlotte replied. "Oh! These young girls of today they have such peculiar ideas," and tried to change the subject.

Elizabeth was relieved when she saw a few friendly faces. Samuel her tutor arrived with his sister Anna, also two cousins from her Mothers side of the family, Emma and Jane who she liked very much. They all had a nice chat before sitting down to dinner. Ada had done them proud with a lovely five course meal. Everyone congratulated Charlotte who announced Ada should have taken all the credit. Later the ladies settled down to play cards while the men stayed in the dinning room to have some port and cigars.

Emily, Elizabeth and her two cousins all played together, and did more giggling than anything else. Emily whispered to Elizabeth. "Did you see Mrs Fitzroy's daughter Louisa making eyes at Edward Hyde it was quite scandalous? Of cause he won't respond to her because he only has eyes for you Elizabeth."

"Emily, I wish you would restrain yourself from saying such things, I have only meet Edward on one other occasion."

"He's so handsome Elizabeth; I bet he asks your Father's permission tonight to call on you."

"Stop it! Emily, please, get your mind on the game, and stop match making."

It so happened that Emily was not far wrong about Edward, every time Elizabeth moved he followed her. In the end she had to give him all of her attention.

When the night was over everyone seemed to have enjoyed themselves immensely. There where

some long drawn out good-byes, but eventually they had all gone. Lying on her bed that night

Elizabeth felt very tired but very happy, it had been a lovely day.

****

CHAPTER FIVE
CHARLOTTE'S DEMISE
****

Everyone dressed in their best apparel on Christmas morning to go to church, it was very warm for late December and the sky was clear blue. Elizabeth wasn't sure if her Mother was up to going, as she'd been feeling unwell for the past week. But Charlotte insisted on going saying the air would do her good. As they walked up the path to the church things seemed strangely quiet.

"Where is everybody today? Asked Charlotte looking around, even the bells were silent. Preacher Goodbody stood in the doorway. "Good morning Mr and Mrs Maybrey, Elizabeth! I didn't expect you today with everything that's happened."

"What ever do you mean? William said looking around the church yard.

"You're not aware that a lot of people in the town are ill with Typhus, we've had eight burials this week."

"Why wasn't I informed of this? William said looking very annoyed. "We lost a couple of people from the mill, but I just thought they had died of natural causes."

"I am sorry you were not informed Sir. Things are very bad at the moment, people are reluctant to venture out of their homes in case they get the illness. There are about six people inside if you would like to join them for the service." Charlotte looked at William. "Well I for one intend to stay and pray for those who are ill and I'm sure Elizabeth will want to."

"All right, I'll be back for you in one hour," said William, "I'm going to see the doctor and see just how serious this thing is. I can't afford to lose any more people, I'll see later," with that he walked away. Charlotte watched him go.

"Sometimes I despair of your Father Elizabeth; it sometimes seems as if all he cares about is that mill."

"He's just worried Mamma, come now lets go in."

Later driving home William warned them that from now on, it would be best if they stayed at home and not venture out until this thing had abated. The doctor had said it was going to get worse, so they would have to think of it as an epidemic and stay close to the Manor. They tried to enjoy the rest of Christmas but it was on their minds all of the time. And by New Year things in the town took a turn for the worse. The death toll doubled, Williams workers were coming down with it one after the other. He tried to get more workers to take their place, but most of them hadn't worked in a mill before, which made things very difficult as they had to be trained. Most of his own workers were only just getting to grips with the new steam power that had been installed. After a few weeks and a lot of trouble things seemed to stabilise and production was on track again.

Soon after New Year they had a visit from Edward Hyde, who was surprised to learn that Charlotte and Elizabeth didn't know he was coming.

Edward's face was a deep red colour as he tried to get the words out. "I'm sorry you didn't know I was coming Elizabeth, I asked your Father for permission to call on you today and he gave his consent. I hope you don't mind?"

"Please don't distress yourself Edward, Its not your fault, Father didn't mention this to me, I think I should have been consulted though. But seeing as you're here, of cause your welcome to stay awhile."

Charlotte went to order some tea from the kitchen, while Elizabeth took him to the morning room. Edward seemed very nervous and kept apologising for turning up uninvited.

"Really it's not important Edward it's nice to have company," she said guiding him to a chair. "Please take a seat; we don't get many people calling on us except a few relations now and then."

"Is you're Mamma keeping well Elizabeth," he said looking extremely red in the face and fidgeting with his collar.

"She hasn't been too good of late, although if you where to ask her she would say she was fine. But thank you for asking."

"I'm sorry to hear that. I suppose you've heard about this illness that's going around.

Terrible thing. My Mother says these illnesses always start in the poorer areas of the town. She said if those people were cleaner things like this wouldn't happen."

"Well Edward it's hard to keep clean when you have four children and can't afford soap, and haven't any coal to heat water to wash them. I'm sure if your Mother thought about things in depth she would agree with me, don't you think."

"Of cause, of cause, you're quite right that's exactly how she would perceive it. You know Elizabeth, your not like most girls I've meet, usually their vain and full of themselves. You're not like that; you seem older than your years. And you are kind and considerate. And I have to tell you quickly, before I make a fool of myself, that I have deep feelings for you. Now I know what you're going to say, that you haven't known me long, I know that! But I hope in time you will come to think of me more than just a friend." Elizabeth looked surprised at his words.

"I don't know what to say to you Edward," I'm very flattered of cause, but as you stated we've only known one another a short while."

"Will you promise me Elizabeth? That you will think about what I've said, and maybe I will be able to call on you again in the near future."

"Yes I'll think about it, of cause I will" she said looking towards the door. A few minutes passed as they talked about the weather and other things. She wished her Mamma would come with the tea. "I'll go and see where Mamma has got to with that tea; I'll be but a moment." Charlotte was sitting in the kitchen showing Sharna how to fold napkins.

"Mamma there you are, I thought you where supposed to be getting some tea? How could you leave me so long with Edward?"

"I'm sorry my dear I thought perhaps you wanted to be alone with someone your own age. Did you have a nice chat?"

"Really Mamma, you're as bad as Emily, if I didn't know better I'd think all of this was a conspiracy to get me married off." she said laughing."

Edward left soon after having his tea; he said he hoped to hear from her soon. Elizabeth thanked him and walked him to his carriage and waved goodbye. She felt sorry for him; it must have taken a lot of courage to say what he'd said. He would make someone a fine husband one day.

Although it was soon after New Year William had gone to the mill as usual. He was a bit worried about how he was going to cope without the full work force. He still had a few things up his sleeve if things got any worse. On returning home that evening he found Elizabeth waiting for him, he got a cool reception from her.

"How could you Father?" she said looking angrily at him. "How could you make arrangements for Edward to call on me without my consent? It was very embarrassing indeed especially for Edward."

"I'm sorry my dear, as you and Edward were obviously getting along so well the last time you meet. I thought you would be pleased to have such a suitable admirer call on you."

"Well what I would really like to know Father is, Why Edward? You did say that he was a partner in his Fathers law firm. I should have thought knowing you the way I do, that you would have somebody in mind for me with a much more higher status."

"It just so happens Elizabeth that his Father is not only a lawyer, he has a half share in a shipping company that exports all over the world. And if I'm not mistaken a few other businesses as well. The family's rich Elizabeth and it could be all yours and Edwards one day."

"Ah! So that's it Father, it's the shipping company your interested in. You said the other day that you were thinking of exporting abroad. This way, it wont cost you nearly as much, isn't that correct?"

"I can't say it doesn't appeal to me Elizabeth, but that's not the only reason I asked Edward to call. He's ambitious as well as being an upstanding person in the community."

"You told me Father not so long ago that if I where to marry anyone, you would prefer someone in the manufacturing business. You seemed to have changed your mind, why is that?"

"You must admit Elizabeth with their wealth combined with ours, all our futures will be secured."

"And what about love for someone Father doesn't that count at all?"

"Of cause it does dear child, the more you see of Edward the more you will like him I'm sure" You're Mamma and I came to think more of one another the longer we spent together."

"But there must have been an attraction for one another Father to start with surely, this has not happened to me. I could never think of marrying Edward, he's a nice man but I have no feelings for him."

"I don't want to hear anymore about this Elizabeth, I've already invited the Hyde family to dinner next week. You're a sensible girl and I'm sure in time you will realise that the most important thing in a marriage is security."

Elizabeth found herself running for the door, slamming it behind her she leaned against it and closed her eyes. How could she have been so naïve, this was her Fathers intention all along. She wondered why he was so intent on marrying her off all of a sudden.

Maybe he was worried he was going to go out of business. Shaking her head she made her way to the library, her Mamma was at the piano.

"Mamma may I have a word with you please ?"

"Yes dear what is it ?"

"Did you know that Father has invited the Hyde's to dinner next week ? For the sole purpose of marrying me off to Edward," she looked at her Mother to see her reaction.

"He has mentioned he would very much like you to get to know Edward more Elizabeth, but hasn't said anything about marriage. Why what did he say?"

"Only that he wants me to marry a man I hardly know, that's all."

"Well I'm sure he has good intentions dear," Elizabeth interrupted her.

"Oh he has good intentions all right, to help himself. The only reason he wants this marriage is because Edwards Father has a half share in an export business. Which will help him export his merchandise."

"Elizabeth I'm sure that's not the only reason, I know your Father a little more than you do. He would never consciously hurt you in anyway. I'll have a word with him tonight to see what his intentions are."

"He's made it perfectly clear what they are Mamma. You will have to tell him that I will not be pushed into marriage. I don't care if they own half of England. When the time comes for me to marry, I and I alone will choose my future husband. I'm sorry to take this stance Mamma, but I have no other choice."

"All right Elizabeth I'll explain all this tonight, I am on your side in this matter you know." Elizabeth put her arms round her Mother. "I know you are Mamma, and I love you for it."

"Things will work out all right dear you'll see. Come, we'll sit in the morning room and have a nice cup of tea. Ada made some tea cakes this morning your favourite."

Later Elizabeth spent what was left of the afternoon at the stables helping John with the horses. She took Ebony to an adjoining field and let her loose. The mare was delighted to be free and ran around the field kicking her hind legs out. They sat on the gate watching her.

"She's such a silly girl, isn't she John? Always doing things you don't expect."

"Its you miss Elizabeth, she's just glad to see you, she'll do anything for you she will."

"When the spring comes john I'll be able to take her out more, then she'll settle down a bit.

John will you put her back in her stable after she's had a good run around the field, I'll have to get back." Elizabeth felt weary as she made her way back to the Manor. It had been an upsetting day; perhaps tomorrow would be a better one. If she only knew that the next day would change her life forever.

Elizabeth woke with a start, what time was it, she must have slept in. Jumping out of bed she dressed as quickly as she could, and made her way down stairs. Mamma must have left her to have a rest; she made her way to the kitchen. Ada and the girls where busy cleaning cupboards out.

"Morning Ada, sorry I'm late, has Father and Mamma had breakfast?"

"Your Father left a while ago Miss, he said to leave your Mamma as she was sleeping peacefully"

Elizabeth looked at the clock it said ten past nine. "That's strange I've never known her to stay in bed this long. She retired early last night complaining of a bad headache. I'll go and see if she's alright," Elizabeth knocked on her Mothers bedroom door.

"Mamma! Are you awake" There was no answer, she opened the door. The drapes were drawn so she drew them back. Walking to the bed she pulled the covers back and gasped at what she saw. Her Mother was soaked in perspiration, her hair was wet and her skin looked grey. There was blood on the pillow which seemed to have come from her nose. Elizabeth shook her gently, there was no response, she tried to scream but nothing came out. Running down the stairs she found her voice and shouted Ada, who came out of the kitchen.

"Good heavens miss whatever is the matter? You're as white as a sheet."

"Ada Mamma is very sick, send Sharna to the stables to tell John to get the doctor. Tell him to take Ebony it will be quicker." Ada rushed to the kitchen shouting instructions to Sharna who got a fright and fell off the stool.

Elizabeth took some cool water and a cloth to bath her Mothers face, Ada wanted to come but Elizabeth stopped her."

"Ada until we know what this is, you had better not come up, I'll see to everything."

"Well if your sure miss, please don't worry to much, it maybe just a chill she's got."

"I hope your right Ada, I really hope so."

Elizabeth sat with her Mother for what seemed like an eternity, then she heard the doctor's voice and gave a sigh of relief. Thank God!.

The doctor looked at Charlotte and told Elizabeth to get a fresh nightgown and a change of bedding. Then asked her to go and wait for him down stairs. She was too scared to ask him what was wrong with her, in case she heard something she didn't want to hear. Elizabeth paced up and down the hallway for about twenty minutes. There was no sign of the doctor. Ada called her from the kitchen.

"Miss Elizabeth, I've sent for your Father, I thought it best, I hope you don't mind?"

"No Ada, you did the right thing, I'd completely forgotten about him. All I could think about was to get the doctor here as quickly as possible. You go and keep yourself busy I'll let you know what the doctor says later."

Elizabeth's Father came through the front door five minutes later, just as the doctor was coming down the staircase.

"Elizabeth, I came as quick as I could. What is it child, what's wrong with your Mamma? Her Father looked very worried. She shook her head.

"I don't know Father I've been waiting for the doctor to tell me."

"Doctor Redmond what's the matter with Charlotte? She was perfectly all right last night," William said looking bewildered.

"I'm afraid its not good news William, she's a very sick woman, I will know in a few hours if she has this cursed illness that's going around."

Elizabeth couldn't believe her ears. "You mean it may be typhus? But how can that be, you said yourself that bad living conditions causes it. We don't have that situation here."

"I know what I said Elizabeth, but since I spoke to you I've had a letter from the institute of Tropical Medicine in Manchester. They have been studying the decease and have issued a paper stating that parasitic lice are to blame. It carries the decease."

"But Charlotte's so clean," William said indignantly."

"You must not reproach yourself over this. This could have happened to anyone of us. She could have been infected anywhere. Now, I'm going to do my best to try and get her better, she will need a nurse. Do you want me to get you one?"

"Yes, yes do that right away please doctor, I want the best there is. If there was something I could do I'd do it, but there isn't," William seemed to be in shock, Elizabeth put her arms around him. "Father I will look after her, I can't just stand around doing nothing I will help the best way I can."

"Elizabeth I know you want to help but its best if you stay away, the doctor knows best what to do. At least until she's out of danger."

"All right Father I suppose your right," she said walking down the hallway to the kitchen. As soon as he's out of the way, she thought! I'm going to help Mamma.

The doctor left saying he'd be back in about an hour. Then her Father left telling Elizabeth he'd be back as soon as he could. She was to wait for the doctor and nurse to come and get them anything they wanted. Soothing her Mothers brow with a cool cloth, Elizabeth spoke to her, hoping she would hear what she was saying. "Mamma were going to get you better, I want you to fight this thing, I love you so much, I couldn't bare it if you left me. She stroked her hair and prayed like she'd never prayed before.

Doctor Redmond confirmed later that day he'd been right about Charlotte, it was typhus. And seeing that she had always been frail, the chances of her getting over this illness were very slim indeed. He said he was very sorry, and he would do everything within his power to help her. This news came as a great shock to everyone, and the fear of who else would get sick was on everybody's mind. The next couple of days seemed to Elizabeth as if she was in the middle of a dream. She couldn't sleep or concentrate on anything; she never left her Mothers side for more than a few minutes at a time. But the care of the doctor and nurse, and herself was not sufficient to save her Mother. Three days after becoming ill Charlotte died in the early hours of Saturday morning, just another name to add to the doctors list for that week.

Elizabeth couldn't believe how distressed her Father was, she could never remember him showing any emotions like he was at this moment. He cried like a baby on her lap, she didn't know how to respond to him as her own feelings where as much as she could bare. Stroking his hair she tried to reassure him that they still had each other, and Charlotte would want him to be strong. In her heart she knew she would never get over losing her Mother. They had never been separated since the day she was born. She had not only been her Mother but her best friend and companion all these years. After a while her Father seemed a little better so she gave him a small whisky from the drinks cabinet.

Leaving him alone she decided to say a last farewell to her Mother. The hearse was coming this afternoon to take her to the church were she was to lie in a side chapel till the funeral. Charlotte looked so peaceful to Elizabeth, as if she were asleep. Bending over she kissed her whispering to her how much she was loved, and how one day they would see each other again. Then blowing her a kiss she left the room and lay on her bed and cried as if her heart would break. After a long while she fell into a deep sleep, not wanting to ever wake up.

People came from all over the county to say farewell to a woman who apparently was admired and loved by many people. To Elizabeth's surprise, a lot of people spoke of how over the years she had helped them out in times of trouble. Charlotte had been very active in the community at one time, but bad health had put an end to that. The last ten years of her life she had devoted herself to her daughter. It had been a pleasant life for the both of them, if only for that short time she was laid to rest under a large sycamore tree in a part of the cemetery set aside for gentry. Elizabeth had a beautifully carved headstone made,

And an inscription stating that here was a woman who had given her life to the town she had loved, and would be remembered with affection by all. She had laid her Mother under a sycamore tree because the old meaning of this particular tree meant persistence, strength and endurance; her Mamma was all of those things in her life. It was hard to leave her Mother there, she sat day after day looking after the grave, unable to admit to herself that she would never see or hear her voice again.

Her Father was never home, since the funeral, he hardly ever left the factory. She thought perhaps he was working so hard to try and forget. This left Elizabeth alone without anyone to turn too. But there was someone who had remembered. As she sat by the grave one day, a voice behind her said, "Hello Elizabeth, I was so sorry to hear about your Mother." She looked up and saw Michael standing there, with compassion in his eyes; it was too much for her. She ran to him, crying, opening his arms he embraced her kissing her hair and tried to reassure her that in time it would get easier to bare.

"I waited for you on Hawks Peak," he said, "Hoping you would come, and I knew you would need someone to talk too. When you didn't come I thought maybe you needed to be with your Father, so I went home."

"I'm sorry Michael I didn't mean to shut you out, I was so miserable I wanted to be on my own. It's been the worst time of my life, I loved her so much, I can't bare the thought of never seeing her again."

"I know how you feel Elizabeth; I felt the same way when John died. All I can tell you is to keep yourself busy and not to be on your own too much. I'll be here whenever you need someone to talk too. It looks as if I'll have plenty of time from now on."

"Why Michael, has something happened?

"Yes, something's happened all right, a lot of workers have been sent home, and I was one of them. There are rumours going around that the recession that was expected has hit all the text stile mills. My Pa over heard Mr Smithfield saying that the orders had stopped coming in, and if it carries on the mill would be in trouble."

"I know nothing of this, Father never mentioned it, although I'm the last one he would confide in. Did they say how long it would be before you got your job back Michael."

"No they never said, I'm just glad the rest of my family are still working, god knows how people will manage if whole families get stopped. Some of them are suffering already with this cursed illness."

"Listen Michael, I'll have to get back there's a lot to do at home. I want you to promise me that if things get any worse for you and your family, you are to tell me, I may be able to help."

"I promise I will, take care of yourself Elizabeth. Will you come to our meeting place on Sunday?"

"Yes I'll be there, I feel so much better now after our talk, thank you for coming," She leaned forward and kissed him on the cheek. He gave her one of his cheeky smiles and waved goodbye. She watched him as he walked away, months ago she had thought of him as a boy, but not any more. He'd grown so tall and handsome, the boy had gone and in his place was a confident man who was coping with life far better than she was. And he also had a lot more to deal with than her. She felt a little ashamed, from now on she would try to pull herself together. She knew her Mamma would want her to go on, and do the best she could with her life. Brushing away the tears she walked through the church yard to where Matthew was waiting patiently with the carriage.

Arriving home Elizabeth went to talk to Ada and the girls, Charlotte's death must have affected them just as much as her. On entering the kitchen she was surprised to see Mary back again, hat and shawl on sitting at the table. She jumped up as Elizabeth came in.

"Please don't get up Mary, I didn't expect you back so soon, I hope your Mother is better now?"

"Yes thank you miss she's well now, I was so sorry to hear about your Mamma. She was very good to me, and I want you to know she'll be missed."

"That's really nice of you Mary thank you. Since your all here together I want you to know that all your jobs are safe as long as I am living here. I know it must have crossed your minds in the last few days, so don't worry, All right." Sharna stepped forward and put her arms around Elizabeth.

"Can I stay here forever Miss? I love being here." Elizabeth laughed.

"Of cause you can stay Sharna, when I said your jobs were safe I meant you as well."

"Sharna! Come away, don't be so familiar" Ada said getting hold of here arm.

"Its all right Ada, she just wanted to be reassured that's all. Has Father been home today?"

"I heard him come in a little while ago. Would you like some tea before dinner miss?"

"Yes please, bring it to the library, he's probably there."

Her Father was standing at the window stirring into the garden. She walked over and touched his arm; he jumped as if his mind was far away.

"Elizabeth! You gave me such a fright, I didn't here you come in."

"You seemed lost in your thoughts. Are you all right Father?"

"Yes I'm all right, I'm sorry I haven't been around lately Elizabeth. I realise you've been on your own a lot, but it just couldn't be helped. I've had so much to do and think about since your Mamma past away. Will you sit down; I have something to tell you. What I have to say to you affects you directly so you have a right to know. I don't know if you have heard or not, but we are having trouble at the mill. The country is in a recession, and by the sound of things its here to stay for a while. This has hit us badly, our order book is empty, and I've had to let a lot of people go. This couldn't have come at a worst time, as you know I've not long introduced new steam boilers into the mill as well as a lot of other equipment. This has cost an enormous amount of money, half of which had to be a loan from the bank. I've thought about this very carefully, and have decided before things get any worse; I would get someone to help us run the buying and selling side of the business. A person who would look at things with a fresh outlook, someone who's had extensive experience in the business world. I thought about getting a complete stranger, but that wouldn't work, what we need is a family member. Since I haven't a son, I've gone for the next best thing. I've decided to ask my nephew James to come to England to join us in our plight. At the moment he's running a cotton plantation in the West Indies, there's just a chance he may like what I'm offering and return home".

As he finished speaking Ada came in with the tea, and Elizabeth poured two cups for them, she handed her Father one.

"What do we really know about this cousin of mine Father? I can't remember you ever mentioning him before."

"Well, as you may know or may not know, my elder brother left for the West Indies years ago and bought a cotton plantation. I used to get some of our raw cotton from him. After a while he married a girl from another family of white settlers and had a son, James. He hadn't been there ten years when he died leaving everything to his son. They managed until James reached eighteen then he took over the place. His Mother always hated living there so she came back to England. It was only quite recently that I heard there was some kind of trouble and he sold the business, we eventually heard he had returned as overseer. Your right when you said we don't know him as a person, but if he's half as intelligent and as good as my brother was he will do us fine."

"Well if it will help you out, I'm sure it can't do any harm Father, it will take some of the worry off your shoulders When do you think he will arrive?"

"If everything goes well he should be here in about two months, then I can spend time at the mill without having to worry about all the other problems."

"Will James be staying with us when he gets here?"

"Well we have all these empty rooms; I was thinking we could put him up in those three large rooms adjacent to the servant's quarters. If you could help me Elizabeth to turn the largest into a sitting room, it has a nice fireplace, it should do nicely. You have a free hand to do whatever you want to them. Don't worry about the money; get some new drapes made and anything else you think might help."

"Mary is back now Father so I will have plenty of help, don't worry, I'll help as much as I can. It will take all our minds off other things …"

"You're a good girl Elizabeth; I don't know what I'd do without you."

"Does this mean from now on I can take full charge of everything appertaining to

Berkeley Grange Father?"

"Yes you will be mistress of this house my dear, I hope I haven't put to much responsibility on your shoulders at such an early age. But I have no other choice."

"Its all right Father, I'm quite capable of taking over this house, I've more or less been doing it for the past few years anyway, trying to take some of the work off Mamma."

"Right that's settled then, I'm quite sure with you taking care of this house, and myself managing the mill, we will be fine. Let's go and have a nice dinner and forget all this for a few hours."

Elizabeth lay in bed that night thinking over the day's events, she was a bit apprehensive about welcoming a complete stranger into her home. She wondered what he would be like, she had forgotten to ask how old he was, well he couldn't be that old being her cousin. He was! Family which seemed to make it easier. Anyway whoever he was if he could help them with the future running of the mill he would be welcome in their home.

Over the next few weeks Elizabeth kept herself busy furnishing the rooms James was to occupy and ordering new drapes for all three rooms. The largest had a nice fireplace and would be perfect as a drawing room. The second was already a bedroom; it had a beautiful oak four poster bed which went well with the panelled walls. The third room had a water closet, one sink and a bath tub. After the rooms had been aired and scrubbed clean, and the new drapes went up Elizabeth stood back and surveyed everything. Yes! That will do nicely; it looked fit for a queen. Everyone had worked really hard to finish everything on time. Even the weather was picking up; spring was on its way. Jo the gardener was busy preparing the beds for the spring planting, and Elizabeth was there as usual to help him. She loved this time of the year, Jo always let her sow the little seeds in trays, it took them a week to do them all. It was lovely and warm in the greenhouse, even after only one week to Elizabeth's delight the seedlings where popping up and reaching for the light. She felt like a new person after the week was up, things had been strained in the

Manor with the worry of that awful disease on their minds. She had kept everyone indoors, nobody was allowed to go to town only Matthew to collect groceries.

Soon he brought the news that no new cases of illness had been reported. He'd spoken to the doctor and he'd said everyone could go about their business as usual that the epidemic was over. This was great relief for everyone; Elizabeth let everyone have the next day off to visit their families. At last she could get out of the house and visit her friends who she hadn't seen for ages. The carriage was brought around and she told Matthew to take her to Monkford Hall. Matthew had kindly given up his day off to take her there. She told him she would make it up to him so he seemed satisfied. She settled back and enjoyed the journey, the fields were still very wet but she could see daffodils appearing at the sides of the road. If only Mamma could see them she thought! She loved the spring so. Wiping a tear from her eyes she continued her journey. Everyone gave her a tumultuous reception when she arrived; they hadn't seen her since the funeral. Emily insisted she stay for the whole day, she didn't resist, it was good to see other faces than those at Berkeley Grange. Emily's mother took her to the drawing room and made her sit by the fire.

"I can't tell you how pleased we are to see you Elizabeth" said Emily's mother. "We get so little company these days with all this illness around. Oh dear! Forgive me dear I quite forgot about your Mamma, I shouldn't have reminded you."

"It's quite all right Mrs Arlington; I would prefer you to talk about her really. I feel that if I keep her memory alive she will be with me always."

"Well you will always be welcome here Elizabeth, remember if your ever in trouble we are here for you."

"Thank you, your so kind, I'm managing really well," And with that she told them about her cousin coming to stay with them from the West Indies.

"How interesting" said Emily, pulling her chair closer to Elizabeth? "I wonder what he's like; do you know how old he is?"

"No not really, I didn't ask Father how old he was."

"You must invite us to the Manor when he arrives Elizabeth, it will give us some excitement in our dreary lives" Emily said grinning.

"You of all people do not have a dreary life Emily. You are privileged in every sense of the word" her Mother said shaking a finger at her.

"Don't you agree Elizabeth?"

"After seeing those poor souls who work in our mill, we are privileged indeed. I give thanks to God every day for what I have. It could easily have been me in their position."

"Quite right," said Mrs Arlington getting up to go and see where the maid had got to with the tea.

When she had gone Emily turned to Elizabeth. "Dear Elizabeth, are you so terribly unhappy after losing your Mamma? I know I would be if I lost mine."

"I feel as if there's a big hole in my life at the moment Emily. I'm hoping in time it will disappear. I still have my Father, and I have good friends which seems to ease the pain."

"Do you still see that boy from the mill, what's his name?"

"Michael."

"Yes Michael. What's he like?"

"He's really nice Emily, and he's been a good friend to me. It's helped to talk to someone who has been through the same thing as I have. His brother died of the same decease as Mamma."

"Aren't you scared your Father will find out about him?"

"No Fathers always at the mill these days and in any case I don't care if he does know. If I'm old enough to run a big Manor like Berkeley Grange, I'm old enough to choose who I associate with."

"Elizabeth, I have something to tell you" Emily said looking very sheepish. "But I don't know how you are going to take it."

"You're my friend Emily you can tell me anything, you know that."

"It's just that Edward Hyde has been calling on me for quite some time now, and we have become quite attached to one another. I know he made an attempt to call on you once, he told me so and you rejected him. He did say he'd been pushed into making advances to you, I wondered if it had been true?"

"Of cause it was true Emily, it was Fathers idea, Oh! I'm so happy for you Emily. I couldn't wish for a better thing to happen."

"You mean it, Elizabeth, Oh I'm so relieved I didn't know if you liked him or not."

"Do your parents approve of the match?"

"Yes they approve wholeheartedly, it may have had something to do with how rich the family is, but I don't care as long as we love one another."

"Well as long as you like him there's nothing to worry about" Elizabeth said taking her hand. "Now relax and enjoy our time together."

The next few hours were spent in the company of happy people which left her feeling so much better. On leaving for home Elizabeth wished them well. They had lifted her spirits, and she was thankful to them for that.

****

CHAPTER SIX
COUSIN'S ARRIVAL
****

At last the day came for her cousin to arrive. Her Father had asked her to give him an hour alone with him, so he could talk business. This seemed quite sensible to Elizabeth so she stayed in her bedroom until Mary came for her. She put on her blue velvet dress and chose a ribbon for her hair to match, she felt quite nervous. This is silly she thought! He is one of the Family isn't he? After a while Mary knocked on her door.

"Miss Elizabeth, your Father asked me to tell you, you may go down now, they are in the morning room."

"Thank you Mary, I'll be down in a minute." She smoothed her gown and made her way down the stairs. Opening the morning room door she was surprised to see not one but two people. James stood in front of the fire with his hands behind his back. A tall slender man handsome in a rugged kind of way. He was dark like herself, except for his eyes which were steel grey enhanced by his tanned skin. The other person was a woman about the same age, strikingly beautiful. She was pale skinned with corn coloured hair, Elizabeth noted how expensive her clothes were, and how confident she looked.

"Are? There you are Elizabeth. Come and meet your cousin James who has kindly offered his services to help us out with the mill. And we also have a nice surprise. He has brought his newly wed wife of three months with him. Catherine is very welcome and is family now . It was quite a surprise I can tell you, but a very welcome one".

Elizabeth stepped forward and offered her hand to James who kissed it, lingering for so long that she pulled her hand away feeling embarrassed.

"I'm sure you are both very welcome here" she said backing away. "We will do our very best to make you as comfortable as possible" James never took his eyes off her which made her nervous.

"You never told me in your letters William that your daughter was such a beauty" looking at Elizabeth up and down.

"Leave the child be James" Catherine said, shaking a finger at him. Can't you see your embarrassing her? Take no notice of him Elizabeth my husband has an eye for the ladies; I have to watch him very carefully". Everyone laughed, but Elizabeth felt uneasy.

"I hope your journey wasn't to tiring. I have your rooms ready if you would like to see them". Elizabeth said walking to the door.

"Don't be in such a hurry dear, I'm sure they would like some tea before they get settled into their rooms" said her Father. "They must be thirsty after their long journey".

"Of cause, as you wish Father. I'll go and tell cook to make some fresh tea".

"And Elizabeth, ask cook if she still has any of those scones she made yesterday".

As she left the room, Elizabeth felt James's eyes following her. It was silly, she thought walking down the hall. Her nerves must be getting the best of her. Tomorrow was a new beginning for everyone. She would make them welcome after all they wont be here forever.

Next morning as Elizabeth drew back her bedroom drapes the sun flooded into the room. Thank goodness she thought, spring at last; I thought it would never get here. She dressed quickly and walked along the landing. Sharna was dusting the stairs.

"Has Father left yet Sharna?"

"Yes miss he left early with the other Mr Maybrey"

"How about Catherine has she come down for breakfast?"

"That new lady had breakfast in bed Miss, I took it to her myself "In bed,

Why? Is she sick?"

"Oh no Miss, she told cook that from now on she was to serve her breakfast in bed". What a cheek, thought Elizabeth. As if these servants don't have enough to do, without waiting on her in bed. I'll have to mention it to Father tonight.

Elizabeth travelled on her own to church on Sunday as her Father had apparently forgotten or didn't wish to go. The mill it seems was first priority these days. Anyway she was happy to go, it did her good to visit her Mother's grave. She would tell her all the news that had happened that week as she tidied the grave. Later on returning home, she spent a while with cook going over the menu for dinner that night, then she went to the pantry and wrapped chunks of cheese, bread and a couple of scones in a napkin, informing cook she was going riding, and would be back in a few hours. She was looking forward to seeing Michael, and hoped he'd remembered it was Sunday.

He was there all right, patiently waiting as usual. As she dismounted he gave her a hug. "Elizabeth I've missed you, have you missed me just a little" he said grinning.
"Yes just a little" she said teasing him, "I've been looking forward to this all morning. Everything back there seems so unimportant to me when I'm here on Hawks Peak. I feel like a bird that's been freed from a cage" she said laughing. You must think me so ungrateful and spoilt, when so many people don't even have enough to eat".

"I don't think of you in that way Elizabeth" he said shaking his head. I think your warm and kind, and the only thing I can't understand is why you come here every Sunday, when you can be with those fine gentlemen in their fine houses. You must have so many admirers".

"No, No, I'm afraid I've led quite a quiet life really. Mamma used to tell me that I must keep my feet on the ground and not be carried away by the promise of money or power. In the end we all need someone who will stand by us in time of need".
"And am I that one Elizabeth? Is it possible that you think of me in that way"?
She looked into Michael's eyes. "All I know is when I'm here with you I'm happy and I feel safe". Michael put his arms around her and kissed her gently on the mouth. "You'll always be safe with me Elizabeth; I will be here as long as you need me. And if it's to be only as a friend then so be it"

It felt so good having him this close to her, the stress she'd felt over the past few weeks had taken there toll on her. She held him for a long time, as if he would disappear if she let go.

"I hope you've brought something to eat with you? He said releasing her I'm starving"

"You're always hungry, she said laughing, how that poor Father of yours manages to feed you I don't know. Sit yourself down I'll get the food. While they were eating their lunch Elizabeth told him all about her cousin and his wife, who had come to stay with them. "What do you think of them" Michael said munching on a piece of bread. "You don't sound too happy they are here".

"Well I'm not quite sure really, they have only been here one day, I don't like to judge people to soon. They are both extremely confident; I just hope they will be able to help Father".

"Well Pa said this recession can't last forever, we can't go back to Ireland that's for sure. Things are much worse there. Coming here was supposed to be a new start for us; we've decided to stick it out. At least for another year".

"I'm so pleased you've decided to stay, I know it can't be easy for your Father. Is there no chance of getting your job back?"

"No, they are letting people go, not taking them on, I've spent every day looking for work, but there's nothing out there".

Elizabeth was deep in thought for a minute. Then jumping up she shouted. "How stupid I am, why didn't I think of it before. You can come and work for me".

"But I thought your Father did the hiring, and besides what could I possibly do? I only know about mill work".

"No your wrong" said Elizabeth getting excited. Father has given me the responsibility of Berkeley Grange. I can make any decision I want, I can hire who I like".

"But what would I do?"

"Well for one thing, you know about horses don't you? You can work with John at the stables, he'll be glad of the help".

"Where would I stay, it's so far from the Town?"

"There's plenty of room over the stables, John is only using two rooms, there's another two empty. What do you say?"

"Elizabeth, I can't refuse, we need the money badly, do you really think it will be all right?"

"Of cause it will be all right, it's perfect, we can see each other every day, say you'll come please

"Yes, Yes, I'll come".

"Good, come tomorrow morning, you'd better make it late, I have to talk to John, and sort your rooms out".

Elizabeth stayed up on Hawks Peak all afternoon; it was lovely feeling the sun on their faces as they rode together. Later they sat and watched the sun almost disappear over the horizon.

"It's been a lovely afternoon" she said standing up, but I'm afraid I must go, I've been here far too long, I'll see you tomorrow about noon".

"I'll be there" he said helping her mount Ebony. "And Elizabeth, thank you for doing this for me, and for coming today".

Leaving Ebony with John she made her way round the back of the house through the rose garden to the kitchen entrance, cook was preparing dinner. She looked up as Elizabeth entered.

"Why Miss Elizabeth, where have you been? Your Father's been looking for you for ages. I've been making excuses for you all day, but I'm afraid he's not in a pleasant mood, you had better go to him at once".

"Where is he Ada"?

"I think he's in the drawing room miss".

On entering the drawing room Elizabeth was surprised to find the atmosphere very cold indeed. James, Catherine, and her Father were having drinks before dinner.

"At last you are here Elizabeth" her Father said. "Can you explain where you have been all day? When I gave you permission to take over the running of the house, I expected you to be here to see to our quests. Catherine has been left all afternoon to fend for herself, do you have an explanation".

"Well I'm sorry Father it I've offended anyone I'm sure. The responsibility of the house as you say is mine. I arranged everything with cook before I left this morning, I had know idea this entailed seeing to Catherine's every need".

"Well, Well, your daughter is not just a pretty face William" James said laughing. "She has spunk. Could it be that our Elizabeth has an admirer? And this is why she is not always at home".

Elizabeth felt her face redden, surely he can't know about Michael, she thought! No he's just guessing.

"Elizabeth would never entertain anyone without my permission" her Father said defending her.

"Perhaps she is finding it to much work looking after this large Manor" Catherine said "If it gets too much for her I can always take it over. As you may or may not know William my Family have always owned very large estates so I am more than capable of managing this one". Before she could say anymore Elizabeth interrupted her.

"I am quite capable of the task thank you; I've been doing it for quite some time. Is that not so Father"

"At the moment we are managing fine, maybe later on Catherine could help you a little. Elizabeth, I'm sure you two ladies will find you have a lot in common when you get to know one another better".

Elizabeth thought for a moment, maybe she had forgotten her manners. She turned to Catherine, "I apologise for my bad manners, there were no bad intentions on my part I assure you".

"I think my wife finds it a bit lonely living in the country" James said taking Catherine's hand. She had a great deal of friends and family in Jamaica. There were parties almost every weekend, so you can understand how it would affect her coming to a new place". "Well it's true we don't mix in high society" said William,

"But we do have some very influential friends. And occasionally we get invites to a few balls".

"Really! How wonderful" Catherine said brightening up. "Can you get us an invite to your next one?"

"I'm sure that can be arranged, we have had quite a few invites since Charlotte died. But with all the trouble at the mill I haven't had time for social events. Now that you are here, I'm sure we can arrange something. It will do Elizabeth the world of good to have an evening out". James came over to Elizabeth and twirled a finger through her hair.

"This I can't wait to see" he said laughing "Elizabeth all dressed up for a ball". Elizabeth pushed his hand away, and felt her face colouring.

"Will you leave that poor girl alone James your always embarrassing her" Catherine said looking annoyed. Just then Mary knocked, and put her head around the door.

"Excuse me sir, cook told me to tell you dinner is ready whenever you are".

"Thank you Mary, tell cook she can start serving right away, I'm sure everyone must be very hungry".

Over dinner Catherine never stopped talking about how wonderful the social life was back in Jamaica, She told of how they used to sit on the porch of an evening after dinner, and the slaves used to sing and dance for them.

"How many slaves worked on the plantation" asked Elizabeth.

"Oh about fifty I'd say, is that a correct figure James?"

"Yes maybe a couple of dozen more than that. It was hard work keeping them in line I can tell you, but they knew who the boss was."

"And what did you do if they stepped out of line? Asked Elizabeth.

"They got the whip that's what; it's the only way of keeping them under control".

"You mean you took a whip and beat those poor souls" she looked over at her Father.

"Elizabeth, this is how things are over there" her Father said looking slightly embarrassed. "It's not England, it's another world."

"I don't care where it is, your own conscience should tell you it's wrong to beat another human being."

"Well high morals may apply to England" said James looking smug. "But over there it's different, civilised people have to take control of those savages else we would all be murdered in our beds. As you grow up Elizabeth you will understand it's a hard world out there. I have known white settlers butchered by those black heathens. You have to make them understand that if they step out of line they will be dealt with severely."

Elizabeth looked closely at this man sitting opposite to her. There seemed almost an element of enjoyment as he spoke. As if he'd taken pleasure in hurting those poor people. There was something about him that made Elizabeth uncomfortable in his presence. Catherine thought the whole thing quite amusing, telling them that James was a wonderful overseer, and could easily take over any business and make it pay for itself in no time.

"Father tells me that the plantation at one time belonged to you James" Elizabeth said looking him straight in the eyes. If it was doing so well, why did you sell it, and later go back as overseer." Before he could answer, her Father said. "Apparently it was beyond his control Elizabeth. There was an uprising, someone set fire to the cotton fields so he sold it and later went back there to manage the place to help the people who bought it."

"I'd had enough of the place anyway James said looking nervous. It was time to come home and be with family again" he said raising his glass. "To the future and to prosperity". They all held their glasses high, Elizabeth looked at her Father he really trusted them, well I hope for his sake he's right, she thought !"

After dinner James and Catherine retired to their living quarters, while William and Elizabeth sat by the fire awhile before going to bed. She apologised to him for being away from the house for so long that afternoon.

"I know Catherine is a lot older than you Elizabeth, but will you try to make her welcome? She must miss her family being so far from home."

"I will do my best father for your sake, but I have to tell you that I feel uneasy about them being here. There's just something I feel, that's not right about them. Will you promise to be careful ?"

"You're bound to have feelings like this dear, your Mother dies and two complete strangers move into the family home. Soon they will feel like family you'll see."

"Father, how much authority have you given to James? Concerning the business."

"James has full authority over every aspect of the business. I was just going to let him have the buying and selling side, but I think he will be able to handle any problem that arises."

"Don't you think it's a bit soon to hand over the mill to him, I'm really surprised you're doing this, the mill is your life, What are you going to do with your time ?"

"Well now that I have a bit of time on my hands I thought I would do a bit of travelling. Maybe visit France to get some textile ideas. It will be a good idea to see how other countries are coping with the climate in today's market."

"But how long will you be gone for" Elizabeth said looking shocked."

"About three months in all dear, not to long, you and Catherine have the whole house to yourselves. I've given James full charge of all the banking, and household accounts so if either of you need anything you just have to ask." Elizabeth looked shocked.

"I thought I was in charge of the house hold accounts Father. You said I could look after this house"

"Of cause you can see to the running of it, but you didn't expect to have the accounts as well, this is up to the men to worry about. You need not worry your pretty little head over such things. All you have to do is enjoy your life and leave everything to us". Elizabeth felt the colour rising in her cheeks.

"How could you Father? Hand over everything to those people. If Mamma was her she wouldn't approve of any of this, and I think you know it".

"Well your Mamma is not here, I'm head of this household and I have to do what's best for all of us, including your cousin and his wife". Now I will hear no more about it, it takes a few days' to arrange my passage to France. I'll expect you to go along with this Elizabeth for all our sakes. This is a good opportunity to get some new ideas for the print shop. I hear there are two mills near Preston that are in the process of closing down. This will not happen to us. I intend to fight to keep ours running".

Elizabeth felt a bit uneasy for making such a fuss, he had all these worries and she wasn't making things any better by complaining.

"All right Father, you go ahead and make your arrangements, I'll see to your packing. I'll tell Matthew to get your travelling trunk down from the attic. Is there anything else you want me to do"?

"No I will see to everything else, now go to bed Elizabeth you look tired. And Elizabeth".

"Yes Father".

"Thank you".

"That's all right Father good night".

Elizabeth lay in bed not able to sleep. Three months without her Father being around, she had been relying on his company since her Mamma died but that had not happened. She felt very lonely, and vulnerable. All the responsibility of the house had been taken away from her and given to this stranger who she didn't trust. She wondered what her Mamma would do in such circumstances. She would probably say, be vigilant and don't lose your nerve. This is your home, you have every right to say and do what you like in it. Yes! That's just what she would say, after all three months wasn't all that long. Michael will be here to keep me company she thought. It will be good having him around, he always cheers me up. First thing tomorrow morning I'll get John to help me with the rooms next to his above the stables. Then she would have to spend the rest of the day sorting out all the clothes her Father wanted for his journey. She couldn't believe how their lives had changed since her Mamma had died. Why! Oh! Why did you have to leave me Mamma? Elizabeth had a sudden overwhelming feeling of anger. Soon tiredness over powered her thoughts and she fell into a deep sleep.

The next morning it didn't take Elizabeth long to get Michael settled in, he seemed thrilled with the rooms. And John was pleased to have a bit of company at last, it wasn't long before they where discussing horses, so she left them to get to know one another. There was plenty to do at the Manor and the time was rushing by. Elizabeth went to find Matthew to tell him to get her Father's trunk down from the attic. He was in the drawing room talking to Catherine. She was instructing him to have the carriage brought round to the main entrance right away, as she was going to Manchester to do some shopping. "I'm afraid Matthew won't be available for at least an hour" Elizabeth said, trying to sound as authoritative as she could. "Father wants him to get his travelling trunk down from the attic as it will have to be cleaned".

"This is most inconvenient" Catherine said looking annoyed. "I told James I would call for him at one thirty. We both have a lot of shopping to do, why can't you wait until Matthew gets back?"

"Because it takes all afternoon to go to Manchester and back, I have to do Father's packing he's leaving any day now".

"Oh very well, I suppose I'll just have to wait. I don't know why you don't employ more servants. I had at least twelve in Jamaica".

"Well you may have been able to have lots of servants, seeing as you never afforded them any wages. In this country we pay people for working". Elizabeth said looking defiant. Catherine mumbled something and stormed past them, as she got to the door she turned and said to Elizabeth. "Oh by the way I've had a word with your Father, I'm to have the girl Sharna as my ladies maid from now on. I'll get her the appropriate attire for her while I'm in Manchester".

"You can't do that! Sharna is far too young; she doesn't know anything about being a ladies maid. whose idea was this" Elizabeth said looking annoyed.

"Actually it was James's idea, he especially asked for her and I agreed. He was only thinking of me, he said I needed help with dressing and someone to dress my hair".

"Mary is a much better choice than Sharna she's much older and has more experience" Elizabeth said looking annoyed.

"Well you have her then; the matter is settled anyway, I'll buy her a nice uniform today, if I ever get to start my journey".

After she had gone Elizabeth through her arms in the air. "That woman, who does she think she is? She's been here a few days and thinks she's mistress of this house. I don't know what Father is thinking of, I really don't". She turned to Matthew. "It's all right Matthew go and get the trunk down and bring it to the kitchen. I'll tell Mary to help you clean it".

"Right Miss, I'll be as quick as I can".

"There's no need to rush Matthew, Catherine will have to wait until we have finished". An hour and a half later Elizabeth had the house to herself; it took her all afternoon to pack the trunk. Exhausted she poured herself some tea Ada had made and sat in the kitchen. The girls where busy preparing vegetables for the dinner that night. She called Sharna over and asked her if anyone had told her about the change of position she was to undertake.

"The new Mrs Maybrey said when I heard the ladies maid bell in the kitchen I was to go find her where ever she was".

"Did you understand what she meant Sharna?"

"No Miss Elizabeth, I thought I was to clean the house and help cook when she wanted me.

"Well let me tell you what it means. From now on, you will be attending Mrs Maybrey as her personal maid. Laying out her clothes, filling her bath, and helping her to dress that kind of thing. If it where up to me I wouldn't put you in this position until you were much older. The one thing that's good about it is that you will be earning more money. And if you ever have to leave here you wouldn't have any trouble getting another job".

Sharna brightened up at the thought of more money. "I'm glad about getting more money Miss. Now I can give Pa more money for food for the other bairns".

"All right it's settled then, go back to your work, and if you have any trouble come and see me and I'll help you ".

"Thank you Miss".

Elizabeth looked over at Ada who was shaking her head.

"I know what your thinking Ada, if it was up to me things would be different. Unfortunately I don't seem to have much to say in my own home".

"She's just a child Miss, young for her years; I think it's too much responsibility for her".

"Well Ada let's see how she copes first before we start panicking. I'm thinking the extra money will help the family".

Elizabeth stayed for about half an hour then left, and as she walked into the hallway the main doors were flung open. James and Catherine came in giggling and making a lot of noise. Matthew walked in after them carrying a large number of parcels. Catherine saw her.

"Are !'there you are Elizabeth, come and help us with these things, there's too many for Matthew to carry".

"It's not Elizabeth's place to carry your parcels Catherine" James said coming up to Elizabeth and touching her face. "She's much to pretty to carry heavy things".

Elizabeth pushed his hand away.

"Your both drunk, how could you conduct yourself in this manner" Elizabeth said and in broad daylight".

"Well listen to miss prim and proper" said Catherine flinging her cloak at Matthew. What you need miss is a man, you've been cooped up in this house to long, what do you say James?"

"I think she would make a perfect wife for any man, and if I wasn't married she would be at the top of my list" he said looking straight into Elizabeth's eyes.

"You are awful you naughty man" Catherine said giggling. I see I will have to watch you very closely from now on" she staggered into the drawing room and fell down into a chair.

"You look as if you've bought the whole of Manchester. Where did you get all this money from? Asked Elizabeth.

"Are that's for me to know and for you to find out" giggled Catherine.

"Well you had better get all this upstairs, Father will be home in a minute, dinner is in half an hour, don't be late. Elizabeth was disgusted with them; they seemed to think they owned the place. Muttering to herself she walked back to the kitchen.

William was late getting home; he had been into Manchester to arrange his passage to France. Elizabeth noted how much better he seemed, she didn't begrudge him this happiness. He had been under so much stress these past few weeks. It was good to see him back to his old self. She had waited to go into dinner with him; James and Catherine had almost finished theirs, and were having a sherry. Her Father chatted to them for a while as he ate, telling them what day he was leaving, it would be the day after tomorrow. He had been lucky there had been a cancellation on a boat leaving for France so he took it. He would take the coach from Manchester stopping half way for the night, and then take another down to Southampton, for the boat to France.

"Don't you worry about a thing William, I will take care of everything" said James smiling. "I'll keep this mill running if I have to roll up my sleeves an do the work myself".

"Thank you James I'm sure you will. I hope you will take care of Elizabeth while I'm away? I don't have Charlotte to rely on now to look after her".

James looked over at Elizabeth. "You can be sure I will look after her, as if she were my darling wife. Elizabeth felt his eyes burning into her, he waited for some reply from her but she didn't raise her head. For the next twenty minutes Catherine talked of nothing but the shops in Manchester. How she was pleasantly surprised how good they were. They actually had the latest gowns from Paris and so reasonably priced.

"My wife is not happy unless she's shopping" said James laughing. "I know how to keep her content, just mention shopping and dangle money under her nose".

Everyone laughed, but Elizabeth thought to herself! I bet she can.

The clock struck nine which gave Elizabeth the excuse to retire, but instead of going to her room she made her way through to the kitchen and unlocked the outside door, and quietly slipped out. It was a beautiful night the moon was full and gave off an eerie light which covered everything. It felt really good to get out of the house; she made her way through the gardens to the stables. Then up the back stairs and knocked on Michael's door, he was surprised to see her.

"I thought I would see if you where all right" she said making an excuse.

"Never been better thanks to you Elizabeth I don't know how to thank you for this, please come and sit down".

"I can't stay long I'm afraid, they just might miss me" she said looking around, "I came because I needed someone to talk too".

Michael pulled a chair out for her," There's nothing wrong is there?"

"No nothing I can put my finger on anyway" Michael sat opposite her and took her hand in his. "Tell me about it, anything you say will just be between you and me".

Elizabeth explained how her Father was leaving for France the day after tomorrow, and how he'd handed over the running of the mill and the Manor to James.

"And what's this fellow like this cousin of yours, you don't seem to keen on him".

"I don't trust him Michael, I'm usually quite good at judging someone's character, and Father doesn't seem to notice anything. Do you think I could be wrong, it could be just nerves on my part"?

"Well I suppose it could be, but you do strike me as the hysterical type, you're the most sensible person I know". You had better be on your guard though just in case. When your Father has gone, make sure you lock your bedroom door a night".

"You don't think he would?"

"No of cause not, but it's better to be safe than sorry".

"All right I'll do as you say. Its so good having some to talk to thank you Michael" she said squeezing his hand. "I must go now before someone locks me out".

Michael took her to the door. "Now don't worry, I'm here if you need me" he said kissing her hand.

"Thank you Michael, I'll see you tomorrow" she turned and kissed him on the cheek. Making her way back to the Manor she felt a little easer knowing she had someone she could turn to. Creeping through the kitchen door she locked it with a sigh of relief nobody had noticed her absence.

The next day her Father and James were in the study all morning, she wished she could hear what was being said. But she had told herself not to interfere, as her Father surely knows what he is doing. So she did what her Father told her to do, and that was to enjoy herself. Going round to the stables she saddled the two horses and went riding with Michael. It was lovely on Hawks Peak; the spring sunshine felt so good, little coloured flowers were poking their heads up between the rocks. Everything seemed to have come alive after a very bleak winter. They sat for a while enjoying the warmth and talking about France and what it would be like to go there.

"Why don't you go with your Father Elizabeth? It would be a wonderful experience. I don't know anyone who has ever been to another country".

"Well I suppose I could have gone if I had insisted, but I didn't want to leave everything in James hands. At least if I'm here I can perhaps watch what he's up too. Anyway let's not talk about them today. How would you like to come and visit my friends at Monkford Hall?"

"I can't go with you to places like that Elizabeth; those people would never accept me into their home".

"Well we will worry about that when we get there, come on it'll be fun" she said dragging him off a rock and towards the horses.

"All right but I'm not going any farther than the kitchen door".

It took them thirty minutes to get to Monkford Hall riding steadily; Michael was amazed at the sight before him. They past through huge gates and rode down a very long driveway. Large rhododendron bushes stood proudly on both sides of the drive. The hall came into view around the third bend. A very large house appeared through the trees, with grey stone turrets that seemed to reach for the sky. To Michael there seemed to be windows everywhere.

"How many people live in this place Elizabeth? He asked in amazement"

"There are four in the family, Mr and Mrs Arlington, Emily and her brother Thomas. Then there are all the servants of cause".

"I think I'd be scared to death living in a place like this" he said his eyes widening. There must be ghosts I'll wager walking around at night". Elizabeth laughed.

"You are funny sometimes Michael, but I can see what you mean. I suppose to you, places like these seem enormous. But when you've lived in them all your life you don't notice anything unusual, it's just home to me. Come now I'll take you round to the kitchen, Mrs Parkinson the cook will give you some lunch. She's a lovely lady and a good friend of mine".

As they entered the kitchen cook ran forward and put her arms around Elizabeth.

"Its about time you came to see me Elizabeth, how are you dear. I was so sorry to hear about your poor Mamma. There! Is a person, who is with the Lord, you can be sure of that. She was a saint that lady a real saint".

"Thank you Mrs Parkinson it's really nice of you to say so".

"It's only the truth dear. Now let me look at you. My you've turned into quite a beauty and no mistake. And who is this with you?"

"He's a friend of mine and a hungry one at that, do you think you could find him something to eat?"

"Any friends of yours are welcome here, come on lad I've just baked some steak and kidney pies for lunch. We'll have some together as soon as I've served the family".

"Are they all at home today? Asked Elizabeth, I didn't notice anyone about".

"Yes dear their all in the drawing room waiting for the luncheon bell to ring. You go through I'll be serving lunch soon".

"I have to take the horses to the stable first, I'll ring the bell at the main entrance, and the maid will let me in".

The family were very happy to see Elizabeth, and where glad she was getting out and about. She told them all about her Father leaving for France the next day.

"You poor thing you'll be all alone in that big house" said Mrs Arlington taking hold of her hands.

"No she won't Mamma Elizabeth has her cousin and his wife living there now, don't you remember".

"Yes of cause Emily I had forgotten, how silly of me. Well you will be alright then, it will be good company for you".

"Yes I'm sure it will Mrs Arlington thank you for your concern".

After lunch Elizabeth suggested a walk around the gardens. "I would love to see how you are planting your flower beds".

"What a good idea" said Emily's mother? You two go ahead, I have a lot of things to see to, I'll see you later". When they where outside Elizabeth told Emily she had brought Michael with her.

"Where is he" Emily said looking surprised.

"Having lunch in your kitchen, you don't mind do you"?

"Of cause not, how exciting! Will you introduce me to him?"

"Only if you promise not to say a word to your Mamma about him".

"I promise I won't, I know I'm a bit of a gossip at times but with you it's different".

"All right, let's go and get him then. Is there anywhere we can go to be alone?"

"There's the weir, I go fishing with Father sometimes it's in the middle of Tarpoly Wood not far from here".

"That sounds perfect let's go".

Michael felt much happier to go with the two girls when he heard there was fish in the weir. Emily borrowed a fishing rod from one of the garden out houses, and then they made their way through two fields and over a stile which led to the weir. It was a truly magical place, very secluded with large willow trees that hung over the water. The shadows they made allowed one to see the fish more clearly as they swam around in its depth. Michael thought it was paradise.

"Why is he so excited about a few fish? Emily asked looking puzzled.

"Because it's food for his family" whispered Elizabeth.

"Oh I see I'm glad I'm not poor" Emily said wrinkling up her nose. "I should simply hate it".

"You would not last two days Emily, without your maids and fancy dresses" Elizabeth said laughing.

"Oh well, I suppose your right. It's such a pity he has no standing in the community. He's really rather handsome".

"Talking of handsome men how is Edward these day's" Elizabeth said changing the subject.

"If I tell you something will you promise not to say anything? Elizabeth shook her head. "He has asked me to marry him, and I have accepted him".

"Why that's wonderful, does your Mamma know?"

"Not yet, he's coming tomorrow to ask my Father's permission, I'm so nervous I can hardly sleep".

"I'm so happy for you Emily, he's a nice man I know you are going to be really happy".

"Thank you, I'm sure I will, you must come to my engagement celebrations quite soon". They stayed at the weir all afternoon watching Michael pull out one fish after another.

Towards the end of the day it started to get a bit chilly so they made their way back to the Hall. Elizabeth thanked them all for having them, and went to collect Michael from the stables. It had been a wonderful day and they left feeling so happy.

****

CHAPTER SEVEN
FIGHTING ALONE
****

The time came for her Father's departure; it was not a happy occasion for Elizabeth. For her Father's sake she acted as if nothing was amiss. The trunk was loaded on to the back of the carriage, she wished him luck, and in turn he told her to look after herself, then he was gone. The Manor seemed strangely empty and cold as she walked down the hall, except for Catherine shouting at Sharna upstairs in her apartments. I don't know what that woman expects of such a young girl she thought! She walked to the kitchen, cook was busy with the baking, and Sarah was helping her. Elizabeth got herself a drink and sat by the fire.

"Is everything all right Ada? Are you managing with the two girls"?

"Oh yes Miss, Sharna comes down sometimes to help me when Mrs Maybrey has to go out. The one thing I can't understand is why they took Sharna out of the room in the servant's quarters, and put her in that empty room next to their apartments, nobody has occupied that room for years".

"You mean they have moved her Ada? Without saying anything! That woman seems to do whatever she wants without telling anyone. I'll go and have a word with her, that child needs people of her own age to talk to; she won't see anyone living in the other end of the house. Elizabeth knocked on Catherine's door and Sharna opened it, she could see at once she had been crying, Catherine called out to her. "Who is it girl?"

"It's Miss Elizabeth".

"Well don't just stand there bring her in". Catherine was sitting with her feet up by the fire drinking tea. She looked at Elizabeth "And what do we owe the pleasure of this visit Elizabeth? It certainly is not to ask after my health".

"Why has this child been crying" Elizabeth said looking hard at her. "What have you said to upset her"?

"Upset her! Why the silly little wench pulled the hair out of my head. I can't believe I'm defending myself, she's just a servant, and I should have given her a good whipping".

"How dare you talk like that in my house" said Elizabeth feeling the blood rise in her face. "You are not in Jamaica now, beating slaves. This is England and we are civilised here".

"How dare YOU !" said Catherine, putting her tea down, "Why you're no better than a silly child yourself".

"I may not be as worldly as you are, but I know when someone is being cruel to another human being. If I ever see, or hear of you laying a finger on my servants again, I assure you, you will be sorry. And whose idea was it anyway to change Sharna's room to your apartments"

"If you must know, it was James's idea, he was only thinking of me in case I needed anything during the night".

Elizabeth looked at her coldly, "You really are a terribly selfish person Catherine, did it not occur to you, that Sharna may need other people to interact with. She will be on her own now at the other end of the house, with only her own company".

"Well if you are going to make such a big thing out of this, I may consider letting her go down stairs in the afternoons. As long as she brings me tea at three o'clock, I can't do without my tea in the afternoon". Elizabeth turned to Sharna.

"Is that acceptable to you Sharna" The little girl nodded her head in agreement and looked as if she wanted to disappear through the wall.

"It's all right" Elizabeth said taking her hand. "Come with me, we'll go and see cook, she has those scones you like with the cherries in. You can come back in half an hour". Catherine walked over to the bedroom and slammed the door, muttering under her breath. As they reached the bottom of the stairs James came in the front entrance, seeing him she told Sharna to go to the kitchen as she didn't want her to hear the conversation.

"Elizabeth, I was hoping to see you today. You're a very illusive person, every time I try to talk to you, you disappear. It couldn't be that you are avoiding me could it" he said smiling.

"I assure you sir, it's not avoidance, and how could it be, as you are never in my thoughts at all".

"Come now Elizabeth, don't play games, you're not averse to a little flattery now and again, I'll wager. All woman like to be told their attractive" he touched curls that had fallen over her shoulder. And in your case beautiful is more the word I would use". Elizabeth pushed her hair back, and started to walk to the kitchen; she turned and said to him.

"Save the flattery for your wife sir, you may need it, something tells me she is not in good spirits today" James didn't answer as he climbed the stairs.

After talking to cook awhile Elizabeth went back into the hall to get her cloak and bonnet then made her way to the stables to talk to Michael. He was busy brushing Major down after exercising him. Michael looked up as she entered.

Hi Elizabeth I hoped you would come today. How's everything?" He said putting the brush back into the bucket.

"Oh, fine thanks, I see your taking good care of the horses they are looking wonderful".

"I've never been so happy in all my life, and it's all down to you". He said looking slightly embarrassed.

"I've done nothing, it's you that's done all the work Michael, the stables have never been better".

"Come upstairs I want to show you something" he said playfully pushing her towards the stairs.

"All right, All right" she said laughing, you go first".

As they entered his room, she noticed he had white washed the walls and made more wooden chairs. It looked really nice.

"You have been busy, haven't you; I must say it looks much better".

"Thanks, I wanted it to look nice in case you came again">

"Well it looks really good, thank you. Now how about you boiling some water for some tea".

"I can't afford tea, will milk be all right".

"Oh, Michael I'm so sorry of cause you don't have tea, milk will do fine really". They sat at the table stirring into the cups, Michael spoke first.

"Your cousin was here awhile ago, asking if anyone knew anything about horses. I told him I knew a bit about them, said he was going to Manchester tomorrow. There's a horse fair on, he wants to buy a couple of good horses for his wife".

"We have perfectly good horses here if they want to go riding, Elizabeth said looking shocked.

"I told him that he said your horses were not good enough".

"The cheek of that man, I know they aren't young but they are reliable".

"He'd been told that there was going to be some Irish bred one's there. He must be after the best, they don't come cheap. I know! As I told you before, my uncle breeds them and makes a lot of money out of them".

"They seem to be spending a lot of money lately Michael. Her buying new gowns, and now he's buying horses. I thought we where supposed to be in a recession. Unless he is as good as Catherine say's he is, and the business is doing all right".

"Well things can't be doing that good" said Michael shaking his head. He's stopped all meals in the mill". Elizabeth jumped up from the table.

"What! Do you mean he's stopped the meals? Are you saying we've stopped feeding everyone completely"?

"Yes Pa said as from yesterday all food stops, only the orphans are getting meals. Pa says they are getting fed because the authorities check up to see if they are being looked after properly".

"How dare he! He can't do that, Elizabeth said looking furious. Those people need that extra food through the winter".

"Well he has, Pa said it's not good at all, there's bound to be more accidents now, he said hungry people can't concentrate on their work if they are hungry".

"Your Father is right Michael; this only goes to proof that James is a heartless man, with no compassion for people who are poor. The worst thing in all this is that I can't help them. Father gave him control of everything. James has the say where the money is to be allocated. I can do nothing".

"If only we could get some money ourselves" Michael said looking glum

"But what's to stop us, you just might have something there Michael, I could raise the money and set up a soup kitchen, or something similar. We could use one of those small buildings in the grounds of the mill. What do you think?"

"Wouldn't he cause trouble when he finds out what you've done?"

"I don't care what he say's. James was given the mill and only the mill. The Manor and all the other buildings on the estate were given to me to look after. While you are in Manchester tomorrow, I'll go to the mill and pick a suitable building, and see if I can get things started".

The following morning James and Michael left in the carriage. Elizabeth saddled Ebony and rode to the mill. The weather was really nice, warm sunshine lingered on the fields making steam rise from the ground; the countryside looked almost dream like. She made her way through the large gates leading to the mill. To the left were three small buildings, the first one was derelict the second empty, the third looked more promising. Someone at one time had occupied it. There was one very large room to the front and another to the back; both had cast iron wood burning ranges with large round rings on the top that lifted off for cooking. There was also a fire place in each room ideal to keep the place warm. Everything needed a lot of work but it was possible to get things back to what it was before. All she needed now was to raise the money. After a while she went to see Mr Smithfield, he was in his office snoozing with his feet on the desk. She closed the door with a bang! He jumped up startled.

"Miss Elizabeth, I didn't hear you knock" he said red in the face. "What can I do for you"

Obviously not" said Elizabeth trying not to laugh. I always seem to catch this poor man at the worst possible time she thought.

"I need at least two men to clean one of those buildings next to the mill Mr Smithfield".

"What on earth for? He asked looking surprised.

"I'm going to open a soup kitchen for the workers, seeing as my so called cousin stopped meals being served to them". Mr Smithfield sat down heavily on his chair, without saying a word.

"Well what do you say? Did you hear me"?

"Oh yes miss I heard you, it's a good thing your doing, and I agree the people in the mill need it badly. But I fear your good deed could fail once Mr Maybrey finds out. He is a fearsome man to cross".

"You must just leave Mr Maybrey to me. This is going to be funded by me. I will tell him I did it alone so you need not be worried about losing your job. Will you help me?"

Mr Smithfield thought for a moment. "Yes I'll help you, and gladly".

"Good man, I'll go over all the things we need, it will take about a week to get things Started, and I'll get you to order everything. Tell them to send the bill to Berkeley Grange". Elizabeth spent an hour with him then left. On leaving the mill she rode into town, and made her way down the main street, past the church and came out into abbot's lane. The second red brick house on the left was Mr Robertson's her tutor's house. She used to love coming here as a child with her Mother. The memories she had were of carefree days sitting under a large apple tree, listening to her Mamma laughing with Samuel. She couldn't ever remember her being that happy at home. Samuel was clearly delighted to see her, and ushered her into the kitchen which was lovely and warm.

"You're just in time to eat some of my mutton stew" he said grinning, made it only this morning. Sit yourself down and while you're eating you can tell me all that's been happening at home. I heard about your Father going to France, how long has he gone for Elizabeth?"

"He did say three months Samuel, but I think once he's settled he won't want to come back here for quite some time".

"I don't think your Father would leave you here on your own for to long Elizabeth. He'll be back before you know it you'll see. I have a feeling you haven't come all this way on your own just to see an old man like me. Is there something wrong up at the Manor you wish to discuss with me?" Elizabeth smiled.

"You know me to well Samuel" she said shaking her head. Elizabeth opened up and told Samuel all that had happened at Berkeley Grange in the last few weeks. He listened to her in silence until she had finished.

"Elizabeth is it possible that your seeing things distorted since your Mamma passed away? We were all terribly distressed about losing her, I more than you'll ever know. You may even feel angry she left you so early in your life".

"It's true Samuel I did have those feelings you talk about, but I'm over all that now. You know I'm not one for making up stories. Will you help me if I need it?"

"You know I'll help you Elizabeth, you only have to ask".

She took a draw string purse from her pocket and emptied the contents of it on to the table. The necklace her Mother had given her for her birthday tumbled out and lay sparkling against the white table cloth. It was a beautiful thing made of gold, jade and clusters of diamonds.

"What do we have here?" Samuel asked looking puzzled.

"Is there any way you could help me to sell this? I need to raise money to feed those people as I explained to you. Father left me some money but it won't be enough".

"Well I can certainly try for you. I know a lot of people with exceptional wealth who would love to own something like this. I'll bring you the money in a few days, will that be all right?"

"Samuel I can't thank you enough, it's good to know I have someone I can rely on". Elizabeth spent another hour with him, and then left, thanking him for the delicious meal. On arriving back at the stables she rubbed Ebony down and gave her some oats and water. It wasn't long before Michael returned in the carriage looking very tired. He waved to Elizabeth. John went out to see to the carriage, while Michael walked towards her.

"Did you drop James off at the house?" she asked looking sorry for him.

"Yes, and I don't ever want to spend so long in his company again".

"Why what happened"

"He treated me as if I was a bit of dirt off his boots. And then expected me to help him pick the best horses for him".

"And did you?"

"I pointed out the ones I liked, they happened to be the dearest".

"Did he buy them?"

"Yes, their to be delivered tomorrow, plus two new saddles, it must have cost a pretty penny I can tell you".

"How can he spend money like this while the mill is going through such a bad time" Elizabeth said shaking her head. "I know if Father where here he wouldn't approve of it".

"Do you think he's spending the firm's money Elizabeth? You did tell me your Father left him in charge of all the finances".

"I can't be sure can I Michael, until Father returns I can do nothing, only keep my eye on him. Oh by the way it looks as if our soup kitchen will be up and running in about a week"

"How on earth did you do it so quick?"

"Mr Smithfield said he would order everything we need. I've found a suitable building; I just need a good cook, someone who's used to cooking good wholesome meals".

"Wait a minute" Michael said getting excited. "I know just the very person you want, it's a neighbour of mine Mrs Cross she would be perfect for the job. "She's had eight bairns and a lazy husband to feed; she can make the most delicious stew out of anything. And she would be so grateful for the money".

"She sounds just what we need. Tell her to come and see me in a few days, things may be a bit more advanced by then. You had better get back to the stables now Michael, there's a lot for you to do before those horses arrive tomorrow. I'll see you about noon".

Later that evening Elizabeth entered the dinning room a few minutes after the dinner bell rang. She had not been eating with James and Catherine, having decided to eat in the kitchen with cook. But on recollection she changed her mind. The closer she was to them the easier it was to keep an eye on them. They were already seated.

"Elizabeth! How good of you to join us" Catherine said sarcastically. Your hostess skills have much to be desired child".

James laughed "Now, Now, Catherine put your claws back in. You must forgive her Elizabeth I'm afraid she's just bored".

"And who wouldn't be bored in this god forsaken place. There's nothing to do but watch the grass grow. I have no friends here, I'll be glad when everything's done and we can go home".

"They are very odd words to use Catherine" Elizabeth said looking puzzled. "When everything's done. What do you mean by that? Catherine looked very flustered, James answered for her.

"What she means is sooner or later the mill will be doing very well, and your Father will have no need for us anymore. When that day comes we a can decide if we want to stay in England or go home to Jamaica".

"Well buying me fancy horses and dresses will never convince me to stay in this place" Catherine said swallowing a half glass of sherry. Elizabeth banged her knife down on the table.

"If you had the life of those poor people who work for us, you would know what hardship is. Especially as they have had even the food out of their mouths taken away". Elizabeth was furious she wanted to jump up and slap her but thought better of it. Catherine looked at James.

"What does she mean by that?"

James rose from the table and walked over to the drinks cabinet to poor himself a drink of whisky.

"I have decided to discontinue serving meals during working hours" he said not turning round. "It's costing the company far too much money, which can be spent on more practical things like fuel for the boilers".

"So you think by starving those poor people you will get more work out of them, is that what you had in mind James ? Asked Elizabeth feeling her face colouring. Because if it is you will be sadly mistaken. The least you can do is to face me when I am speaking to you" James turned and sat at the table again.

"You must understand Elizabeth that we have to save as much as we can to get the business back on track. We have to make savings somewhere! Anyway, they get paid for their work don't they? There lucky to have employment, mills are closing down all over the north of England.

"Well you will not get away with starving the people in my mill" Elizabeth said looking defiant. "I have made other arrangements to give each and every one of them a meal at lunch time. And before you ask, I will be funding the whole operation, so you don't have to worry about them any longer". Elizabeth waited for his reaction. He was quiet for a minute.

"And where may I ask did you get the money to fund this idea of yours" he said, stirring at her coldly.

"That's my business" she said turning and looking him straight in the eyes. "Surely you can't have any objection to this? Seeing as it wont cost you a penny piece".

She was surprised at the answer she got back, she expected opposition to her plans but instead he turned away laughing.

"Well, I have to hand it to you Elizabeth you certainly got one over on me this time. Go feed your workers I have no objection, I like a woman with spunk. It's a pity Catherine wasn't more like you, we would be a force to be reckoned with".

Elizabeth gave a sigh of relief. "You had better get Catherine up to bed James I fear she has had too much to drink"

James took his wife's arm and pulled her up out of the chair "Come to bed Catherine before you fall from the table. Elizabeth is right you are drunk" Before leaving the room James turned to her. "I have invited a few friends over tonight to play a few hands of cards. We will try not to disturb you, goodnight"

She wondered who these men where that were coming. Oh well it had been a long day, and she was tired, it would do her good to have an early night.

After spending a good hour seeing to her toilet and brushing her hair, Elizabeth walked to the window and opened the drapes and looked out. The moon was full and bright and a shimmering light lit the whole of the garden terraces. She could hardly drag herself away from the scene which had a calming affect on her. Laying in bed she soon fell off to sleep but was awakened a few hours later by a door banging. Must be those men leaving she thought! Turning over she tried to go back to sleep. Suddenly she could hear footsteps coming along the landing, they stopped outside her door. The knob on the door started to turn slowly; she could see it clearly as the light from the moon lit up the whole room. Someone called her name, she new at once it was James's voice, he sounded drunk. "Elizabeth! I want to talk to you" he said rattling the door knob. "I know you can hear me open the door. After a while he seemed to give up, she heard footsteps walking away from the door. Sleep was impossible to achieve after this but towards morning she fell into a deep sleep and it was ten o'clock before she woke. Dressing, she went down the stairs, Ada was in the dinning room with Mary, and she sounded very agitated. Opening the door Elizabeth was met with a sight she could hardly believe. The room was in a terrible mess. There where empty ale bottles, smashed glasses, and food laying everywhere. The dinning room table was burnt with cigars, and one of her Mothers favourite vases lay broken on the floor.

"Miss Elizabeth whatever happened here last night "Ada said throwing her arms in the air. Do you know who made this mess?"

"I'm so sorry Ada, James had some people here last night I don't know who they where, but after this I don't think I want to know. Can you manage to clean it up all right? I'll help you if you like".

"You'll do know such thing miss it's not your place to do such things, Mary and I can manage. You go to the kitchen, there's some fresh tea on the hearth, we won't be long".

"Thank you I'll do that, where are the girls?"

"Sarah's doing the brasses, as for Sharna I haven't seen her since yesterday afternoon".

Later after she'd had her breakfast Elizabeth went to check the servant's quarters. It had been quite a while since she'd gone into that part of the house. Everything seemed clean and tidy. Just as she was going to go back down to the kitchen she heard Catherine
 shouting. She turned around and went to see what the trouble was. Catherine was standing in the doorway of Sharna's room pointing her finger in a threatening manner. She stopped as she saw Elizabeth.

"I wish you would do something with this lazy child" she said. "I can't get her out of bed, say's she's sick, just a ploy if you ask me. I want her to help me try on my new riding outfit, James has promised to take me riding after lunch".

Elizabeth couldn't believe this woman, she seemed to have no thought for anyone's feelings.

"Did you not think that Sharna may be ill and need our help? Elizabeth said. "You will just have to manage to get dressed yourself. I'll see to her now GO!

Catherine mumbled something about these English needing a few lessons in how to run a household, turning she walked away. Elizabeth took no notice and went into the room and sat on Sharna's bed. She was very flushed and wouldn't look at Elizabeth.

"What is it dear? Don't you feel to well? She said stroking her hair. Sharna shook her head, "Would you like me to send for the doctor" Sharna sat up and put her arms around Elizabeth. "Please don't send for the doctor, I don't like them. You won't will you ?" Elizabeth was taken aback how upset she was. "Of cause I won't if you feel that strongly about it. I'll assign Mary to look after you for a couple of days,

The tears rolled down Sharna's face. "Thank you miss, will you think about putting me back in my old job please? I hate it here please"

"Yes I will think about it I promise, know try to get some rest. I'll send Mary up with some nice hot soup for you".

After making arrangements to get Sharna settled, Elizabeth spent half an hour with cook then made her way to the stables. James was there helping Catherine saddle one of the new horses. They were beautiful animals but Elizabeth thought they were to highly strung. If one wasn't used to such animals they could be dangerous. Catherine was her usual self, complaining about everything. The saddle looked uncomfortable; the horse didn't seem to like her. In the end James had had enough, he picked her up bodily and through her into the saddle.

"For god sake woman stop complaining, I lavish everything upon you and still you're not satisfied".

Michael was standing next to Elizabeth and whispered in her ear. "Those horses are not fit to ride without proper training, there to wild. He may be able to handle them but she won't. You'll have to stop them somehow".

Elizabeth didn't want to get involved but thought she had better say something. Shouting to James she said. "You can't let her ride that horse she'll kill herself". He had already moved outside the stable. He turned to Elizabeth and shouted. "Keep out of this; it's got nothing to do with you". Just as he said it Catherine's horse reared up, she fell over backwards on to the ground. Michael ran forward and caught the reins. Catherine's pride was a little dented but she wasn't hurt just shocked. She yelled at James saying she would never ride another horse as long as she lived. And stormed off towards the Manor rubbing her backside. He shook his head and pointed to Elizabeth.

"How about you Elizabeth, mount up and show her how to ride a horse, come with me it'll be fun". She turned her back on him and didn't answer. "Well please yourself" he said, then whipping his horse he galloped across the yard and through the gate.

"He's trouble that one" Michael said shaking his head. You'll do well to stay away from him". Elizabeth didn't say anything to him about the night before; he was in no position to tattle James

"Don't worry Michael; I stay as far as I can from him. Now it's a lovely day, saddle up the horses we will go to Hawks Peak. I'll get Ada to do us some lunch, bring the horses around by the kitchen door in ten minutes".

It wasn't long before they where settled in their usual spot on Hawks Peak enjoying some newly backed pies that Ada had made. Michael thought he was in heaven.
"This is the life Elizabeth, what could be better than this, warm sunshine, lots to eat, and a view like that. Why would anyone want anything else?" Elizabeth laughed.
"To you and me Michael it is everything, but there are some people who are never satisfied. Catherine for instance, nothing is ever right for her". Michael started to laugh.
"Did you see her come off that horse? The funniest thing I've seen for a long time". Elizabeth saw the funny side of it to and couldn't stop laughing.
"We shouldn't laugh at other people's miss fortune really we shouldn't" Elizabeth said trying to control herself. "But she did deserve what she got; I don't think she will be complaining for a while".
Elizabeth told Michael that Sharna was not too good at the moment. She had instructed Mary to look after her till she was better.
"I didn't know she was sick, are you sure she's all right" he said looking concerned.
"Yes she should be better in a few days, don't worry we will look after her".
"Thank you for that, she's not like a lot of people, she's a really sensitive person who needs a lot of attention".
"Yes I have noticed that, Ada will keep an eye on her there's no need to worry". Michael jumped up and grabbed Ebony's reins.
"Can I have a ride before we go I love riding her?"

"Of cause you can, you don't have to ask, give her, her head a little I think she'll enjoy a good gallop". Michael disappeared over the hill and was out of sight for the next ten minutes. Just as she was wondering where he had go to, he came walking over the hill leading Ebony. James was riding one of the new horses. As he got nearer he shouted to Elizabeth.

"Did you give this stable hand the permission to ride this horse? Elizabeth looked at him defiantly.

"As far as I can remember that horse belongs to me, not you, I can lend it to whoever I like".

"You should be aware of your place in society Elizabeth, consorting with stable hands doesn't become you". Elizabeth grabbed Ebony's reins.

"I'm quite aware that you and your wife think you're above everybody else. This is my land and I'll do whatever I please on it, including consorting with stable hands" James looked at her curiously.

"You're getting very upset over something as trivial as a horse Elizabeth. It couldn't be that this boy here is more to you than just an employee, could it?" Elizabeth froze, if I let my guard down now she thought! Michael will be in bad trouble.

"How dare you sir, suggest such a thing. But of cause I wouldn't expect anything else from the likes of you".

James pointed the whip at Michael. "Stay in your place boy or you'll feel this whip on your back" He looked at the picnic cloth on the ground. "Enjoy your lunch" he said sarcastically. Turning he rode away. Elizabeth saw Michael's face, and scared he was going to go after him she grabbed his arm.

"Don't Michael, PLEASE! He stopped and turned away kicking a rock in temper. "I'm sorry about all this Michael; I should never have put you in this position. We will have to be very careful from now on. Come, let's go back" Gathering up everything they made their way home.

As Elizabeth walked back to the Manor the young delivery boy was dismounting his horse with a letter in his hand. He shouted to her. "Letter from Monkford Hall I'll be back tomorrow for the reply" He ran forward tipped his hat and put the letter in her hand. Elizabeth opened it; it was indeed an invitation to attend Emily's engagement dinner. It also included James and Catherine, she wondered if she could get away with not telling them. But as the thought entered her head she dismissed it at once. It would never work, James knew the entire well to do families in the area, and he'd made it his business to get to know them. She had been amazed at the information he had gathered about them in the sort time he'd been here. She would tell them tonight at dinner.

Elizabeth kept busy all day; she went to see how Sharna was. Mary told her she hadn't eaten anything today as she had slept a lot.

"All right Mary leave her to rest, if she isn't better by morning I'll get Doctor Redmond to look at her".

"Right miss, Oh, by the way, Mr Robertson has arrived; I've put him in the library".

"Thank you Mary, will you make some tea and bring it in?"

"Right miss, would you like some cake with that?"

"Yes please, see if cook has any of that seed cake left Samuel always enjoys that".

Samuel was busy rummaging through the books in the library; he looked up as she entered.

"Are there you are Elizabeth, I hope you don't mind me delving into your books? You have such a wonderful selection".

"You know you can take anything you want from this house Samuel. As far as you're concerned I consider you one of the family" she said grinning at him

"That's the nicest thing you could have said to me" he said walking forward and kissing her on the cheek. "By the way I have the money for you from the sale of that necklace" He took a pouch from his pocket and handed it to her.

"You didn't have any trouble selling it then?" she asked.

"Good heavens no! Are you satisfied with what I got?"

Elizabeth looked in the pouch "Samuel, it's more than enough, thank you for doing this for me. You may have saved a few lives by your action. Now sit yourself down,

Mary's bringing some tea and some of that seed cake you like so much ".

"Well it was worth the journey up here to sample Ada's cake" he said settling himself into an arm chair by the fire.

They both spent the next two hours discussing books and talking about old times. The library clock struck six as Samuel was putting the books back on to the shelves. He said he'd have to go before it got to dark. Elizabeth asked him if he'd received an invite to Emily's engagement dinner, he said he had, so she said goodbye and she'd see him then. That evening at dinner Elizabeth told James and Catherine about the invitation she'd received from the Arlington's of Monkford Hall. Catherine was highly delighted.

"At last I can wear one of my new dresses she said beaming. We will show these English nobles what real class is. Before my family went to Jamaica they had bigger houses and more land than any of them".

"Oh, you're such a snob Catherine" Elizabeth said shaking her head. "There are other things in life besides money and status. This dinner is special; it's to celebrate Emily's engagement of marriage to Edward. It's not an invitation to see who is clad in the best finery". Catherine pulled a face.

"You're such a bore Elizabeth. Don't you want to have the good things in life, fine dresses and jewellery? I thought every woman wanted those things".

"I think Elizabeth could achieve all those things and more if she put her mind to it" James said looking at her. "She's turning into a real beauty".

Elizabeth avoided his eyes but felt them as they moved over her. She shivered and making some excuse left the room. As she walked to the kitchen tears swelled in her eyes. How could you Father, she thought! How could you leave me to face this on my own? It was supper time in the kitchen, everyone was sitting at the table, they all seemed in good spirits. Telling everyone to carry on, she sat by the fire, it seemed the only place lately where she felt relaxed. The laughter felt good, she remembered how her Mother and herself enjoyed being here laughing with everyone. But soon enough she was brought back to reality when Mary addressed her.

"Sharna will be up tomorrow Miss Elizabeth, I told her if she didn't feel any better by tomorrow the doctor was coming to see her. She soon perked up, said she would be ready for work tomorrow".

"Thank you Mary I'm glad she's alright".

After the dishes were washed and the kitchen was tidy, Elizabeth told them to go to their rooms and thanked them for working so hard. She made her way into the hall and locked the main door. As she was ascended the stairs James came out of the library. She thought he had retired earlier.

"Elizabeth, can you come into the library a moment? He said, seeing her hesitate he said. "Only for a moment". She turned and followed him in.

"I hope this wont take long" she said I'm very tired. He guided her to a chair.

"Please sit down Elizabeth; I assure you I don't bite. I'm sorry you're uneasy in my presence, for I only have the highest regard for you. I've watched you for a long time now, and have been very impressed with the way you have handled yourself. It couldn't have been easy excepting strangers into your home, after losing your Mother". He paused and looked away. "I wanted to ask you something, have you thought of your future at all? Your Father won't live forever, and when he goes you will be left with the responsibility of the mill, and in this day and age only a man will be taken seriously as to the running of a mill".

"Well, I will worry about that when the time comes" she said indignantly. "Father is healthy and has no intention of retiring our dying. And why would you be so interested in my future. This is only a temporary position here for you and your wife. As soon as my Father returns I presume you will be going back to Jamaica?" Elizabeth jumped as he grabbed her arms.

"To hell with Jamaica. Don't you know it's you that I want, it's driven me mad being so near to you and not telling you how I feel. Don't tell me Elizabeth you haven't felt it too?

"I don't know what you're talking about" she said struggling to get free from his grip. "I have not given you the slightest notion that I was interested in you. I could never bring myself to look upon a man such as you. Especially a married man".

"But I'm not married to Catherine, that was just a ploy to make society except us on our return to England. I could never marry someone as sensitive as her, she would drive me mad". Elizabeth looked shocked.

"Does she know you have no intention of marring her?"

"No of cause not. Don't worry about Catherine she will one day latch on to someone else who will give her everything she wants. She would leave in a minute if the right person came along". Elizabeth went to walk towards the door, she felt so disgusted with the whole affair. James tried to block her way.

"Please don't go Elizabeth; I want you to hear what I have to say. For a long time now I've had you on my mind. I was hoping in time you would come to like me. I would love you and take care of you, and as time past you would come to except me as your husband". Elizabeth looked at him deeply; it was no wonder women were attracted to him. He had a self assurance and charisma that was attractive to them. But she could see through the façade, he was cold and calculating, and she prayed god would give her the strength to rid herself of this man before he destroys everything that she holds so dear. "I don't know why, you think I would one day accept you as my husband James. I have not got the slightest affection for you, and could never think of you in that way. Any man, who would disgrace a woman's name by pretending to be married to her, must apparently be lacking in morels. You would certainly be ostracised from the community if they found out". James looked decidedly uneasy.

"You wouldn't do that Elizabeth it would mean the business would suffer, and you know what that means"

"Yes I'm quite aware what it would mean" she said defiantly, and you also know that I could never tell anyone for that very reason". James took her hand and looked into her eyes. "I could change for someone like you Elizabeth; just say the word and I'll be anything you want me to be". She opened the door and turned to him.

"People like you don't change James; you've had my answer now please leave me alone".

James called to her as she started to climb the stairs.

"It's that stable hand isn't it, it's him you favour" Elizabeth went cold, turning to look at him she said. "Even if it where true, which it is not, it would be my business and nobody else's". Tossing her head in defiance she climbed the stairs. There was no response from James, sighing with relief she went to her room and closed the door.

The next week was very busy for Elizabeth. The soup kitchen was harder to organise than she thought. Mrs Cross came to see about her job, Elizabeth took her through all the things she would have to do. Mrs Cross seemed to think that with a bit of organisation she would be able to manage all right which was a great relief to Elizabeth. She promised her she would get her two young helpers, which pleased her very much.

"People in this town wont forget what you have done for them Miss Elizabeth. You've saved so many from starving. I heard there are people in Manchester dying like flies after those two mills closed down. Yes, people won't forget this in a hurry".

"Thank you Mrs Cross it's nice of you to say so".

"It's only the truth miss".

"Well I can leave you to see to everything from now on. If you need anything it doesn't matter how small, call on Mr Smithfield he has promised to assist you in anyway he can".

"Thank you miss I wont let you down".

"I'm sure you won't Mrs Cross, and thank you. I'll call in soon to see if you're managing all right". It was a great relief to Elizabeth to finely let somebody else take over the worry of the soup kitchen. With everything else on her mind this was one worry she didn't need.

Elizabeth tried to stay away from James and Catherine the next few days only spending time with them at dinner in the evening. James was very quiet and hardly addressed her. As for Catherine she was continually asking her about the invitation to Monkford Hall.

Had she got the date right, what kind of people where they, was it true Monkford Hall had over sixty rooms. Elizabeth informed her that yes! It was true; it was a very large Hall. It had been a monastery back in the sixteenth century, but when they were abolished by King Henry the eighth, it was taken away from the monks and given to the Arlington family for their support of the crown. Their ancestors used to attend court in those days. And do today. Catherine was beside herself with excitement.

"Well that makes them nobility then" she said smiling from ear to ear. "Did you hear that James. We are going to dine with real noblemen; at last we can finely meet well bred people". Elizabeth just shook her head and left the room muttering to herself. She heard James laughing.

"Look what you've done you've chased Elizabeth away. Arlington does attend court still today on and off, mostly he's in London attending to other business's he has. But I agree he is very influential". Elizabeth walked down the hallway wondering where James got his information from so quickly.

****

CHAPTER EIGHT
THE ENGAGEMENT DINNER
****

Mary, Mary, Aren't they ready yet? Called Elizabeth standing at the foot of the staircase. "The carriage is here".

"They are nearly ready miss" Mary shouted from the top of the stairs, "Two minutes".

"How long does it take to get dressed" said Elizabeth exasperated. "It's three hours since they went to their apartments. Tell them we are going to be late".

A few minutes later James and Catherine made an appearance. Elizabeth was speechless when she saw them. Catherine wore the most beautiful gown Elizabeth had ever seen. It was obviously French, made of pink silk with the latest bustle at the back in white. In her hair she wore a pink feather held down with a diamond hair clip. James also looked very distinguished in a new attire. Catherine looked at Elizabeth.

"Well what do you think? Do we, or do we not do justice to this household".

"Yes, "Yes, you look very nice" Elizabeth said, "Now please go to the carriage. Matthew has been waiting outside in the cold".

"Oh let him wait, really Elizabeth I don't know who is in charge of this place, you or the servants". James opened the door and led them to the carriage.

"Now, Now, ladies, let's not squabble tonight. We have a very pleasing night in front of us, so let us go and enjoy it".

It was a beautiful night, clear skies and every star seemed brighter than the next. Elizabeth would have enjoyed the spectacle if Catherine hadn't gone on, and on talking about things that had no interest to anyone. James eventually stopped her with one sharp word.

Elizabeth apologised to everyone on their arrival for being late. Emily and her family gave them a special welcome, and took them into the drawing room to introduce them to everybody. They all wanted to know who the beautifully dressed couple where. It wasn't long before a circle of people stood around them. Catherine seemed to be loving every minute of it. Emily pulled Elizabeth out onto the terrace, she seemed very excited. "You never told me how interesting this cousin of yours was. How tall and handsome he is, and his wife is exquisite. That gown must have cost the earth. All the women are swooning over him. You're so naughty not introducing them to us sooner".

"Well they are very charming in public, but I assure you Emily there is something not quite genuine about them, nothing I can prove yet, but I'm keeping an eye on them, I don't trust them".

"You know Elizabeth these past few months have been hard for you. But things will improve as soon as your Father gets back from France. I'm sure you will feel much better then you won't feel so lonely". Elizabeth realised that Emily would not be able to understand the situation, so she changed the subject.

"Here I am going on about my troubles and we should be discussing you and your engagement to Edward. I'm so happy for you Emily you look so radiant, when is the big day? Soon I hope".

"In about three months, it will take that long to organise everything. Oh! Elizabeth I'm so happy, Edward is so kind and generous I feel so lucky to be marrying him".

"You are lucky sweet dear Emily and I wish both of you every happiness" Emily hugged her. "Thank you Elizabeth you are a darling". "Now come inside and enjoy yourself this is your night" Elizabeth said with tears in her eyes. As they entered the room James came over to them.

"There you are " he said taking Elizabeth's hand. " I've been looking for you, the dinner bell has rung would you let me escort you to the dinning room" Elizabeth nodded and placed her hand on his arm. The dinning room was a sight to behold; the table glittered with beautiful silver candelabra's and cutlery. Spring flowers sat in crystal bowls along the full length of the table. They had taken a lot of trouble with the slightest detail. Everyone congratulated the hosts on their table, Mrs

Arlington looked very pleased and thanked them and hoped they all enjoyed their meal. Elizabeth sat next to Emily, James and Catherine were opposite them. They seemed quite at home and chatted to everyone as if they had known them all of their lives. Catherine never stopped talking about Jamaica she answered many questions about the place. Elizabeth noticed James touching her arm and trying to change the subject. But it seemed to be too late as Richard Hyde Edwards Father overheard the conversation.

"Are! We seem to have something in common with one another James" Edward's Father said addressing him. "I visit Jamaica every couple of years. Where did your lovely wife say you had your plantation?"

"It was ten miles outside Kingston I don't think you will be familiar with it".

"But of cause I know where it is, exactly. It's that big whitewashed house right on the river. Quite a place. Wasn't there a big rumpus not so long ago, I believe the slaves rebelled and a few of them where shot". Elizabeth looked at James he had gone quite white. Everyone went silent waiting for his reply. It seemed ages before he spoke his words came out in a stammer.

"Oh! That, that happened after I sold the place. You'll have to ask the new owners about that one". Elizabeth stirred over at James she had never seen him so flustered before. He was always so calm nothing every scared him, but this had. And I bet I know why Elizabeth thought, it was him who killed those poor people. Maybe they asked for their freedom and he refused them. I remember Father saying once that slavery had been abolished but it would take years for the owners of these plantations to take notice if every of the law. It would seem those people finely found out they where entitled to their freedom. She was so deep in thought she jumped when Emily spoke to her.

"Your very quiet Elizabeth are you all right?"

"Yes, Yes, I'm fine really, thank you Emily".

"You have hardly eaten anything is it not to your taste?"

"The food is delicious I guess I'm not very hungry. Tell me Emily where are you going to live after your marriage to Edward?"

"Well Father wanted to buy us our own home, but after a word with Edward and considering the state of the economy, we thought it would be more sensible to have the west wing of Monkford Hall as our home. There will be a little furniture to buy and some drapes but that is all really. It seems silly buying a separate home when we have all these rooms empty".

"I'm so pleased Emily, now I have more people to visit, and in time I hope you'll allow me to be godmother to all those little ones I hope you and Edward will have".

"Give me time please" said Emily looking embarrassed. As she finished speaking, Mr Arlington rose from the table and addressed everyone.

"I hope you all enjoyed your meal as much as we have enjoyed having you all here tonight". He went on to congratulate the couple on their engagement, and welcomed Edward into their family. And was quite certain they would be very happy in their new life together. Everyone raised their glasses and wished the couple health and happiness. After a while the men retired to another part of the Hall, while the ladies settled in the drawing room. Elizabeth started to relax and on the whole enjoyed the rest of the evening. People started to depart around eleven o'clock, so they decided to leave also. After saying their farewells to everyone they made their way home. James and Catherine never said a word on the way home. And Elizabeth didn't care enough to ask them if they had enjoyed the evening. It took a long time to reach Berkeley Grange because there where a lot of clouds obscuring the moon, everywhere was pitch black. Matthew relied on the horses to guide him; they always seemed to know their way home. Finely they arrived home. Elizabeth went straight up stairs as she was very tired, it had been a long day. As she got to her bedroom she could hear James shouting at Catherine. It wasn't unusual she thought! They were always arguing lately, closing the door she locked it and went to bed.

Two months past, and conditions at the mill were bad, but not as bad as others. So far thirty two workers had lost their jobs. Elizabeth had given orders to the manager that anyone they let go would still be entitled to receive meals from the soup kitchen, until things picked up and they got their jobs back. She hoped that her Father would send a message somehow, maybe through one of the sea captains whose ships docked at Southampton. But no such letter arrived. On Sunday after church Ada called her into the kitchen.

"Did you want to talk to me Ada?"

"Yes miss, I don't want to trouble you, but I thought I'd better tell you I've been having a lot of trouble with the deliveries of food. And since your Father owns the main grocery shop in town I thought I'd better mention it".

"What kind of trouble Ada" Elizabeth asked looking puzzled.

"I believe they are having trouble getting supplies. Mr Hughes who manages the shop has told me that the supplier's haven't been paid for two months, and are refusing to deliver any more goods. If things don't change he will soon be out of stock."

"Well I thought things where going too smoothly" Elizabeth said shaking her head. Can you manage for a little while Ada? While I see what's going on".

"Yes miss, we should be all right for a little while longer. There is a problem with the delivery of flour from the local mill too. They haven't been paid either".

"Good lord! What is that man thinking of, he can't even do a simple thing like paying the local trades people. Don't worry Ada I'll try to put things right, carry on and I'll talk to you tonight".

Elizabeth sat in the dinning room reading a book on one of the window seats, when she heard the carriage pull up. The main doors were opened and she could here James's voice. She went into the hall; he looked surprised to see her.

"Elizabeth, what's this, I thought you would out on a lovely day like today with your little stable hand". She felt the blood rushing to her face but managed to control herself.

"Well at least I have friends in the community which is more than I can say for you".

"And what may I ask does that mean" He said raising his eyebrows

"I believe that not only have you not paid supplier's who deliver to our grocery shop, but that the local flour mill hasn't been paid either"

"Oh is that all, I though you were talking about something serious".

"Of cause it's serious" Elizabeth said getting angry. "If the shop has nothing to sell, people will starve. Haven't you done enough damage to the town's people without taking away what little they have left? Don't you realise that shops like that are the heart of a community, not to mention the profit we get out of it, even if it is a small one"

"You know Elizabeth; you should distance yourself from the likes of those people. God put two kinds of people on this earth, those who give orders and those who take them. If you get too personal with them they will take you for everything you have".

"Good god man, do you think by starving people they will work harder for you. If you do, then I'm sorry for you. This is not Jamaica, and these are not your slaves who can be whipped into submission. Now are you going to pay the supplier's or not?"

"I've never seen you so fired up Elizabeth it suits you. You should get angry more often it makes you even more beautiful than you already are" He made to come towards her but she put her hands up in the air.

"It's alright" he said backing away. "I'm not going to touch you. I'll tell you what, come riding with me this afternoon and I'll pay those supplier's your so worried about"

"Never, said Elizabeth turning away".

"Well if that's the way you want it, so be it" he started to climb the stairs and as she reached the library she looked back and said to him.

"All right I'll go riding with you, but don't think it's anything else but that". James nodded smiling to himself.

"I'll see you around three o'clock then at the stables" he said and walked up the stairs. Around noon she called at the stables and told Michael to meet her by the river in half an hour after she had spoken to Ada. Making her way to the kitchen she went to enter the rose garden when she heard voices and noticed James talking to somebody who was partly hidden by the bushes. Pressing herself against the wall she waited till he turned and went around to the main entrance. As the other person came into view she recognised him as Mr Scarsfield from the apprentice house. Then he was gone.

What on earth does he want with a person like that, she thought! Although it didn't surprise her for one minute at the company he keeps. On entering the kitchen the smell of bread baking made her feel hungry. She sliced a small loaf that had been baked earlier and put some smoked ham between the slices. Wrapping them in a napkin she told Ada she would be back in two hours.

"Oh before you go miss, something has to be done about Sharna. The girl is not herself lately she comes down to help me in the afternoons like you arranged. But all she seems to be doing is crying all the time and I can't get any work out of her".

"I'm sorry to hear that Ada, I'll go and see her after I get back".

Elizabeth and Michael sat by the river soaking in the warm sunshine eating their lunch.

"I've never been this happy in all my life" Michael said taking her hand, I wish this could go on forever".

"There's no reason why it shouldn't go on forever" she said laughing. "As soon as Father comes home things will be different. He'll be so glad to be rid of those two up at the Manor he will accept you as a trust worthy friend and you will be welcome in our home".

"Haven't you heard from him in all this time Elizabeth?"

"No not a word, if I know my Father correctly he will turn up unannounced as large as life, giving his orders as usual. Enough about me, how is your Father managing at home, are the children all right?"

"Father is still working at the mill seems he has a bit more knowledge than the rest of the men on his floor. He was saying last night if it wasn't for that, he would be out the door".

"I'm very glad for them Michael it will be one less worry for you. Although Ada tells me she is having problems with Sharna".

"What kind of problems?

"I haven't had time to find out yet, I'm going to see her when I get back. If she's very unhappy as a ladies maid to Catherine I'll bring her down to the kitchen and I'll ask Mary to do her job instead. She's a nice girl she won't complain. I've been a bit worried about Sharna for a while but I just haven't had the time to see to her".

"I know your doing what you can for her and I thank you for that".

"Michael, I'm going riding with James this afternoon, I thought I'd better tell you". Michael jumped up and through his arms in the air. "You can't do that, this man may be dangerous".

"I only said I'd go because he has more or less threatened to hold money back. Money that should be going to pay suppliers that deliver to our shop in the town. I will be all right really; it's more than he dare do to lay a finger on me. It's just a ride that's all ".

"You promise me not to dismount, or walk with him on your own".

"I promise, now stop looking so worried. When we get back, you had better saddle Ebony and one of the other horses, so I can get it over with".

Later after their ride Elizabeth went to find Sharna, she was just coming out of Catherine's apartments with her.

"Are! Elizabeth I'm going in to Manchester to do some shopping. James say's he has a meeting this afternoon, so you can have this lazy little madam. I'll be back about six o'clock; the maid can come back then".

Elizabeth shook her head and took Sharna to her room. They both sat on the bed.

"Now dear" Elizabeth said stroking her hair. "Sit down and tell me what's troubling you? Ada tells me you're not at all happy". Sharna burst into tears and through her arms around her.

"Good heaven's it can't be all that bad what is it?"

"Please miss take me away I can't stay here please".

"Well if you're that upset about it you can come back down to the kitchen, would you like that better".

"Oh yes, Oh yes, thank you miss" she walked the door, "Now, can I go now?"

"Sharna it can't be today, I'll have to make arrangements with cook, and I'll have to talk to Mary to see if she is willing to attend Mr and Mrs Maybrey as ladies maid. But I promise I'll move you tomorrow".

"Tomorrow will be to late, please let me go now, please".

"Now don't be silly, it's only a matter of one more night, I'm sure you can manage that". Sharna didn't say another word she walked over to the bed and lay down with her face to the wall. Elizabeth walked to the door. "I promise you, you can go back to your old job in the morning" There was no reply so she went to her own room to get changed into her riding clothes. James was at the stables waiting for her, he gave her a big smile. "I'm glad you came, let me help you on to your horse".

"There's no need, that's what Michael is here for" she called him and he came over. She whispered to him. "I won't be long I'll make it as quick as I can". They rode through the gate and into the lane.

"Where would you care to ride Elizabeth? You no the best places".

"I think we will stick to the roads I don't want to go far".

"Nonsense, we can't give the horses a good gallop on these roads. The only good place is Hawks Peak, we'll go there".

"No, I don't want to go there it will take to long"

"You promised to ride with me remember, are you going back on your word?"

"Oh all right, but I can't stay up there to long. There are things I have to see to at the Manor today".

"That's a girl, relax, for heaven's sake, you'll enjoy the ride it's beautiful up there".

He was right it was beautiful there, all the spring flowers were out and one could see for miles around. The horses were pulling on their reins so they let them gallop for a while. It wasn't long before she was out of breath, pulling up, she said to Ebony "That's enough girl I'll have to rest". James dismounted and came over to her.

"Let me help you down we'll rest here for a while". Elizabeth shook her head.

"No James we had better make our way back" she said remembering what Michael had said. James stretched up putting his hands around her waist and quickly lifted her out of the saddle, on to the ground.

"I'm not going to eat you Elizabeth, stop struggling" he said letting her go.

"I told you I wanted to go back, we have nothing to say to one another you and I".

"Elizabeth why are you so hostile towards me, what have I done to you to make you dislike me so much. You must know by now I adore you, there's nothing I wouldn't do for you".

"This was all a ploy to get me up here wasn't it" she said backing away.

"Please don't be like this Elizabeth we can have a wonderful life together you will come to like me when you know me better just give me that chance".

"You and I can never be together James, I keep telling you but you don't listen. Now let me go or you will be sorry".

"You Will! Be mine one way or another" he said grabbing her hands and pinning her against a large rock. She shouted at him.

"Let me go, let me go, you'll be sorry when my Father gets back, he will whip you within an inch of your life".

"Your Father's never coming back. Do you hear! He was on his way back from France when his ship hit another vessel. It sank and only a few were saved" Elizabeth stirred at him in shock.

"You're lying, how dare you say such things. He'll be back any day now"

"No Elizabeth, I tell the truth, I intercepted a messenger three days ago on the road from Manchester. Apparently there was an early morning fog as they left France. Most of the people on the other ship survived, but not so with your Father's ship".

"You knew this, and you never said a word for three whole days" Tears streamed down her face as she struggled to comprehend what was being said to her.

"Don't cry, don't cry" he said holding her close. Suddenly there was a loud cracking noise. James gave a cry and jumped back. Looking up she saw Michael, he was riding Major and he had a whip in his hand. He had used it on James, who stood there holding his cheek and making a groaning sound. Elizabeth had never seen Michael as angry as he was at this moment.

"Touch her again, and I'll kill you" he said grabbing her horse's reins and waiting until she was mounted. James pointed at Michael

"You'll be sorry for this boy; your days on earth are numbered. One way or another you're dead!" Elizabeth couldn't remember getting home. He took her to her room and she lay down.

"Are you alright" he said touching her forehead.

"You shouldn't have done that Michael he will never rest till he gets his revenge".

"Don't worry about him, I can handle myself. Just let him try again and he'll be sorry he ever set eyes on you". Elizabeth explained what James had told her about her Father.

"Do you think he's telling the truth Michael, can it really be true? Why would he make up such a thing?"

"Well there's only one way of finding out. Do you have someone you can trust? Someone who can make enquires for you".

"Yes, there's Samuel my tutor I trust him with my life".

"Tell me where he lives I'll go and see him and explain what's happened" Elizabeth told him where to go and warned him to be careful.

"Lock your door when I'm gone, I'll be back as soon as I can" he said opening the door.

"Don't come back here Michael I'll see you down by the river in two hours Is that enough time".

"Yes that's fine, now lock this door".

It was five o'clock before Michael made an appearance, Elizabeth was just about to go back home when he came over the hill. She had to wait a moment while he got his breath. "I thought you would never get here. Did you find the house?"

"Yes, I found it quite easy. Your tutor seemed very concerned about you. He told me to tell you that he would leave for Manchester first thing in the morning. And will come to see you tomorrow afternoon when he'd made the enquiries".

"I don't know how to thank you Michael, it's good to know one has such good friends".

"Do you want me to come back to the stables Elizabeth? I can understand if you want me to leave".

"Of cause I don't want you to leave, I'm just scared in case James seeks some awful revenge on you ".

"Don't worry I've had worse things happen to me in my life. I'll just stay out of his way".

"Well if you're sure, we had better start walking back". Michael put his arm around her shoulders.

"Don't worry too much about your Father; it's all probably a terrible mistake. We won't know the truth till Samuel gets back tomorrow".

"Yes I'm sure you're right, I'll try to put it out of my mind till tomorrow".

"Good girl! That's the way, and what ever tomorrow brings we will face it together".

Elizabeth never went down to dinner that night, the thought of facing James was too much for one day. She went to bed early and prayed to god to send her Father home safely.

She was woken the next morning by someone running along the landing. Looking out of the door she saw Catherine at the far end waving her arms in the around.

"What ever is the matter" Elizabeth said looking puzzled.

"I'll tell you what's the matter, that lazy maid has not turned up, I need her to help me dress".

"Is she in her room Elizabeth said shaking her head?"

"Of cause not, that's the first place I looked".

"Well I'll go and see if she's in the kitchen, I can presume you can manage a few minutes on you own" Elizabeth said sarcastically. Sharna was nowhere to be found, her bed hadn't been slept in and all her belongings were still there. Elizabeth searched the grounds with Mary but there was no sign of her. She had to tell Michael she was missing, he was very concerned.

"She's probably gone home last night" he said, "don't worry I'll find her. You go home you have enough to cope with".

"Thank you Michael, I hope you find her good luck".

Two hours later Michael was back, and with him his Father who looked very worried. They waited in the kitchen while Ada went to fetch Elizabeth. She could see at once that they hadn't been able to find her. Michael introduced his Father who apologised for his daughter leaving so suddenly and without telling anyone.

"Please don't apologise, we all think the world of Sharna. Have you no idea where she could be?"

"No, she didn't go back home, it's just not like her, she's a good girl, she has never done this kind of thing before".

"I'm really sorry Mr O'Shea I wish there was something else I could do" Elizabeth said looking upset. I'll tell you what if she doesn't turn up in the next two hours; you had better inform the police. They may be able to help you".

"Yes your right miss, we'll do that then, thank you foreseeing us ".

"Let me know what happens and if there is anything else I can do".

"We will good day".

Elizabeth felt completely drained of energy when they had gone, she went to lie down for a while and didn't intend to sleep, but it came all the same, and with it dreams of ships floundering in high seas and her Father stretching out his arms to her. She woke with a start and wiped the perspiration off her forehead. She knew then that what James had said was true, her Father wasn't coming back.

Elizabeth had been right; as soon as Samuel entered the room she knew by his expression that the news wasn't good. He took her hands and sat her down.

"I've been to the shipping line and they have confirmed one of their ships sank leaving France. Your Father was on board, there were only a few survivors, I'm so sorry Elizabeth, I thought this was the only way to tell you". She sat there for a minute not saying a word.

"What's happening to this household Samuel" she said with tears in her eyes. Everything is falling apart. First Mamma now Father, it's as if the devil himself has taken possession of this house. Now I find out one of our maids has completely vanished. I don't know where it will end".

"What do you mean vanished?

"I saw her last night she was upset at having to stay with Catherine as ladies maid. So I told her that this morning I would let her go back to her old position in the kitchen. I should have realised how upset she was. You don't think she would do anything silly do you?"

"Like what! Oh no, you must not think like that, she'll turn up. But I'm worried about you Elizabeth all this worry is going to have a big affect on you. Do you want me to ask Doctor Redmond to prescribe something for you, a sleeping draft perhaps?

"No really Samuel I'm alright, at least I know the true, and Father is not coming back. I will have to face up to it just as I did with Mamma. As she turned to face Samuel the tears ran down her cheeks. He walked over to her and put his arms around her.

"Cry little one, don't' be afraid of letting go. You won't be able to face this just yet it's to soon, I'll be here to help you, we all will". Elizabeth wiped her eyes and looked out of the window.

"It's not just about me Samuel; it's all those people at the mill. They are all relying on us for their livelihood, if we fail to keep the mill running; I hate to think what might happen to those poor people".

"But your cousin seems to be running the mill alright, well as far as I can see he's doing alright, unless you know something I don't".

"No, there is nothing I can tell you that will discredit him in any way. Other than stopping the distribution of food at the factory. But as you know I found a way around that. And a few bills were not paid. The only thing I have noticed is they both spent an awful lot of money. I also feel as if I'm a lodger in my own home, can you understand that?"

"Yes dear I can, but unfortunately as things stand with your Father gone, nobody will take you seriously if you try to take over the mill. If you have some proof that your cousin is doing something untoward then maybe you will be able to discredit him and take control of the mill. But you will have to find someone to run it until you marry".

"Do you think it would work? Why didn't I think of that, I could go and see the bank manager, he may be able to help. I don't know how, but it will be a start".

"Elizabeth is there anything you wish me to do before I go?"

"There is one thing Samuel, will you go and see preacher Goodbody and make arrangements for a special service to be held for Father next Sunday? If that's possible".

"Oh cause dear child I'll go on my way home, is that all you want?"

"Yes thank you. You have been a great help to me Samuel I won't forget it. Come, I'll get Matthew to bring your carriage around, and thank you again. She waved him off and walked round to the stables to see if Michael had returned. He wasn't there so she helped John groom the horses; it would take her mind off things at least for a little while.

Half an hour later he turned up and by the look on his face Elizabeth could see he had had no luck finding Sharna. He waved his arms at her.

"She's nowhere to be found, we have been to the police they are sending out a search party straight away. Pa is in a bad way I have to stay with him until we know for sure what's happened to her".

"I'm so sorry Michael of cause you must be with your Father. I want you to take my horse, it will help you get around, and you'll be able to search much quicker".

"Thank you, it will make things a lot easier. I'll see you tomorrow, he saddled Ebony and left.

****

CHAPTER NINE
NEWS AT LAST

****

They found Sharna's body early the next morning in the river; she was tangled in amongst reeds under a bridge close to town. People in the town were very shocked, it was one thing dying of illness, but this was a healthy little girl who everyone knew and liked very much. Elizabeth went to see Michael and his Father at their home. They welcomed her in, Elizabeth was surprised to see how they where living. There was just a table and three chairs in the room. An old rocking chair and a cupboard stood at the other end of the room with a few items on it. It felt cold and damp, no fire burned in the grate. Sitting around the table nobody said a word; the feeling of sorrow was so intense. Michael's Father broke the silence.

"It's good of you to come miss, everyone has been so kind, I'm sorry I haven't anything to give you to drink ".

"Please don't bother yourself really, I only called to give you my condolences and to see if I could help in anyway. I feel as if I am partly responsible, as Sharna was under my care".

"No, No, you must not think that, she thought the world of you. Every Sunday when she called from church she talked of you constantly, how good you were to her. I can only think that she must have walked down to the river for a walk and some how slipped and fell into the water. It's a fast running river she wouldn't have stood a chance to getting out".

Michael was very quiet Elizabeth took his hand.

"Are you alright ? You haven't said much". He looked at her with tears in his eyes.

"I can't believe she would have gone down to the river on her own. Don't you remember Pa, in Ireland when she was little, we took her down to the sea, and she was terrified of the water? She was the only one who wouldn't go near the water".

"Yes I remember that" her Father said shaking his head, "But she may have got over her fear, I don't know. It doesn't matter now, we have lost her. Only god knows why he took her".

"What did the police say about it? Asked Elizabeth, " Are they satisfied it was an accident".

"They seem to think it was, but they also said she would be examined by Doctor Redmond tomorrow to establish the cause of death. Elizabeth felt as if she was intruding so she decided to go.

"Pa why don't you go and collect the bairns from Mrs Cross. I will see Miss Elizabeth out".

"Yes I'll do that son. Thank you for coming miss we appreciate it".

"That's all right Mr O'Shea; let me know if you need anything, anything at all". After he had gone Michael told Elizabeth he hadn't mentioned her Father's death as it would have distressed him more than he needed to be".

"I quite understand Michael you both have enough grief to deal with".

"I'll tell him tomorrow, he's not too good today. I'll have to stay till after the funeral if that's all right".

"Of cause, I have a few things I must see to in Manchester I'll see you again soon". "Thank you for coming Elizabeth, Oh ! By the way I've returned Ebony to the stables thanks for letting me borrow him".

"Thank you for that, I hope your Father will be all right, I'll see you soon". He took her to her carriage and waved goodbye.

The next morning the police constable arrived and took a few details, asking them when they had last seen the maid. And did she seem different in anyway. Catherine was sent for and seemed genuinely surprised at the news. She was asked if the maid had been upset about anything. Had anything happened that she would be aware of. Elizabeth watched her closely, Catherine looked very uneasy and her face coloured.

"I don't know I'm sure" she said looking flustered. "All I know is that the girl didn't come to my apartments like she usually does" She turned to Elizabeth "I sincerely hope you don't think that I had anything to do with the child's death ?"

"No, No, mam" the constable said looking nervous, "Nobody's suggesting that. These are just routine questions we have to ask. I won't trouble you any more, thank you for your help, if we need to speak to anyone else I'll let you know, I'll see myself out". Catherine was very quiet; she went into the morning room and closed the door. It was obvious to Elizabeth she didn't wish to talk about what had occurred. Making her way to the kitchen Elizabeth asked Matthew to bring the carriage to the main entrance. Soon she was on her way to Manchester. It was a lovely sunny day, but she hardly noticed because of an overwhelming feeling of depression. It wasn't long before the hustle and bustle of the Manchester streets came into view. To Elizabeth everyone seemed to be rushing here and there as if life was about to end at any minute. She had never liked the city to much, and was always glad to get back home. Matthew knew where the bank was as he had taken her Father there quite often. They pulled up at the door and she went inside. The interior was quite impressive, high ceilings sloped down to beautifully carved woodwork and panelled walls. On the floor patterned tiles weaved there way along the full length of the building. She felt a bit intimidated as the bank was full of men. They all turned and stirred at her as she made her way to what seemed to be the main office at the far end. A teller saw her and came around to open the door.

"Can I help you miss" he asked. Elizabeth tried to control her nerves,

"I would like to see the manager please, my name is Elizabeth Maybrey" Inside the room she heard a voice say to him. "Its all right Henshaw, show the lady in" Elizabeth walked in and was greeted by an elderly gentleman with very white hair and a beard to match. He walked over and shook her hand.

"Well ! I didn't expect such a lovely lady to honour us with her presence today." he said smiling at her. "My name is George Harrington I'm the manager here how can I help."

"It's good of you to see me I didn't know if I had to make some sort of appointment".

"No its quite all right my dear, I do know who you are, and before I say anything else I want to tell you how sorry we all were to hear about your Father" he guided her to a chair. "He was a good man and he will be sadly missed".

"Thank you it's kind of you to say so. I presume my Father saw you before he left for France to make arrangements for my cousin to take over the business while he was away"

"Yes, he did make such arrangements, your cousin was to have full access to both accounts, a savings account and business account. I have been trying to contact Mr Maybrey for two weeks now, but have had no reply. I'm afraid the loan that your Father took out with us has not been paid for those two months. I'm sure there is a good explanation for this, but I just wanted to make sure that it would be paid soon. As it was stated in the agreement, it has to be paid on the first of every month."

Elizabeth was visibly shocked. "I'm so sorry to hear that Mr Harrington, I to hope there is a good explanation. Is it possible for me to have access to these accounts ? Being that I am, or will be soon the rightful owner of my Father's business".

"I'm afraid that's not possible my dear, at least not until your Father's will is read".

"I don't even know if my Father left a will Mr Harrington, I just haven't had the time to go to the lawyers to find out".

"Well, I strongly advise you to go as soon as possible, and then you will have a better idea on where you stand in all of this. You should know your rights, or you will find people taking advantage of your vulnerable position".

"You are quite right Mr Harrington; I've been so distressed these past few months I haven't given enough attention to my future. I'll go directly to the lawyers today, I don't know how to thank you, you have been so kind".

"Think nothing of it my dear, I always have time to talk to beautiful young ladies such as yourself" he said winking at her. Smiling at him Elizabeth shook his hand. "Thank you again good day".

Leaving the bank she told Matthew to go straight to Hyde and Sons and wait for her. Mr Hyde senior greeted her warmly.

"Elizabeth, come in, come in. I really am so terribly sorry about your Father. I haven't got in contact with you because I thought you needed to have time to yourself before talking about business matters".

"Well Mr Hyde I have really only come to see if my Father had left a will. It had completely slipped my mind, but I would like to know now".

"You mean you haven't spoken to James Maybrey about the will, he told me he would speak to you about it yesterday. It's to be read out tomorrow here in this office".

"No sir I was not told about this. He's been to see you about this matter then ?"

"Yes he has been to see me on several occasions. I'm sorry you were not notified about this matter. I only made a point of telling him first as your Father had left him in charge of the business"

"I can understand that of cause, but I am the rightful beneficiary of my Father's business. And subsequently I wish to be informed on every matter appertaining to it".

"Why of cause Elizabeth, and you will be, I assure you. There wasn't any intention on my part to keep things from you. I will be opening the will tomorrow morning at eleven o'clock. And if there is anything you don't understand I will be only to happy to assist you in any way I can".

"Well I have a feeling I may need your services again in the near future". Mr Hyde looked surprised.

"Oh, can you be more pacific my dear ?"

"I can't say at the moment, I just hope that if I call upon you to help me, that you will be happy to do so".

"Oh cause dear child, you can rely on me to help you in anyway I can. Your Father was a good friend to me and I won't forget it".

"Thank you" she said walking to the door. "I'll see you tomorrow at eleven o'clock good day"

Returning home Elizabeth felt exhausted and went to lie down for a while. She must have drifted of to sleep but was woken sometime later by someone shouting.

There was an argument going on between Catherine and James. She was yelling at him and telling him in no uncertain terms that she had had enough of living in this god forsaken country. And she was going back to Jamaica on the first available ship. Elizabeth didn't quite catch what James replied; what ever it was she didn't like it. The next thing was, bags and suit cases were flung on to the landing and Catherine was yelling for Mary to help her. Elizabeth thought it best to stay out of it, and subsequently went down to the kitchen for a drink. Mary ran past her muttering. Elizabeth could hardly believe at last she was getting rid of one of them. There was a slight chance that James would follow her. An hour later she walked down the hall; all Catherine's bags had been brought down and put by the main door. Poor Mary looked red in the face with all the packing she'd had to do. Elizabeth told her to go and tell Matthew to bring the carriage around to the main door. James stood at the top of the stairs grinning as Catherine came down the stairs her eyes were very red.

"Where will you go ? Asked Elizabeth looking from one to the other.

"I shall go to Liverpool and await a ship going to Jamaica".

"But that could take weeks Catherine you don't have anywhere to stay".

"Then I'll find somewhere" she said indignantly. "I know how long I will have to wait, I don't care, I can't stay another minute in this house with that man".

Matthew came in and looked around.

"I don't know if I can get all this lot on Miss Elizabeth", he said shaking his head.

"Please try Matthew; I'm sure you will find the room somewhere".

Soon it was time for her to leave, all Elizabeth felt was relief. She helped Catherine into the carriage. As it pulled away Catherine leaned out of the window and said to Elizabeth. "Watch him closely Elizabeth he has a taste for pretty girls especially young maids". Elizabeth wasn't quite sure what he meant, although she had expected some kind of last minute sarcasm towards him. Entering the house she saw James going into the dinning room, she followed him in; he was pouring himself a drink. He looked up and saw her. "Elizabeth, come and sit down, would you like a drink ? I hate to drink on my own". She ignored him and sat by the fire.

"You don't seem at all upset about Catherine going like that" she said "didn't you have any feelings for her at all".

"Catherine was a gold digger Elizabeth, she would have left in an instant if the right person had come along. As far as I'm concerned she's done us all a favour by leaving". Elizabeth looked at him, what a cold nature he seemed to have she thought. She didn't think for one minute he could have feelings for anyone.

"Why didn't you tell me that the will was being read out tomorrow morning"? She said coldly, waiting for his answer.

"I'm sorry about that" he said "I simply forgot".

"James why did you come to England ? Was it to do with what happened on that plantation? You must have been very relieved when you got Father's letter inviting you to come to England. It was a quick and easy way out of the situation you found yourself in. I'm right am I not"? Elizabeth nearly jumped out of the chair the way he ran at her. "Why you little minks, you think you're very clever don't you ? He said with his hands on the arms of her chair and his face right up to her's. "I came here to help your Father out of a bad situation. And it doesn't matter if he's here or not, that's just what I intend to do". Elizabeth pushed him away and stood up.

You're a liar, do you hear, a liar" she said feeling the anger surging though her body. "You came here with your so called wife to deliberately talk your way into my Father's affections, so you could get your hands on the business. I know now why you wanted to marry me, you have no affection for me, I mean nothing to you. But you under estimated who your dealing with, you of all people should know that the Maybrey's are fighter's and I am no exception. You will never be master of this house; I will fight you all the way". James took hold of her arms.

"My dear child do you think for one minute that you can run this enormous estate and business by yourself, you would be laughed out of town. Business men won't take you serious; you would be bankrupt in no time. You need a man like myself to take charge. Don't let your emotions cloud your mind Elizabeth. Think of what will happen to all those people who rely on you for their livelihood. Your Father spent years building his business up, what do you think he would say if he was here ?"

"Of cause he would be on your side" she said pulling her arms away. "You convinced him that this family meant something to you. But I know different, and I am going to prove it somehow".

"You really are paranoid Elizabeth, I think you should go and see your doctor. You need to go for a rest somewhere. By the sea perhaps, it will do you good".

"How dare you talk to me like that as if I was losing my mind" she said shaking with emotion. I have no intention of going anywhere. The person who is going to leave this house is you" She left the room slamming the door hoping he hadn't sensed any fear in her.

The next morning Elizabeth sat in the kitchen having breakfast with Ada when Matthew came in to say Doctor Redmond and a policeman had just arrived, and wanted to see her. She quickly showed them into the morning room. By the look on their faces she realised something was wrong. The constable spoke first.

"I'm sorry to disturb you so early miss, but the doctor and I have some news about your maid that died. We thought you would want to be informed about it."

"Of cause constable what is the news you have ?"

"Well it seems after the good doctor here had examined her, he found that the girl was at least two months pregnant. Now for her family's sake we have kept this silent from the town's people. Her father is an honest hard working man and we don't want to cause him any unnecessary grief. He has been notified of this, and as you can imagine he is very shocked". Elizabeth couldn't quite take in what they were saying. Tears appeared in her eyes as she turned to the doctor.

"Are you quite sure about this Doctor Redmond you couldn't be mistaken could you ?

"No Elizabeth" he said shaking his head "There is no mistake".

"But she was a good girl; she would never have done anything like that. And she certainly wasn't street wise like a lot of the girls in the town. Her brother informed me she was a brilliant scholar, and a kind and gentle sister to him".

"Did she go out at night after her duties where done ? Asked the constable.

"Well I can't keep track of the comings and goings of my staff, this is a large house, and I try my best to see they are comfortable and happy in their work. But in Sharna's case I know she never left this house, only on a Sunday to go to church and to visit her family".

"I'm sorry I have to ask these questions" the constable said looking uneasy. "I hope you will understand the reason why I'm asking them".

"Of cause I understand why they have to be asked constable. I only wish there was more I could tell you" Elizabeth turned to the doctor.

"Do you think she could have known of her condition?"

"No Elizabeth I'm quite sure she didn't know".

The constable took out a note pad and asked Elizabeth to name everyone who resided at Berkeley Grange and how long they had worked there. After writing it all down he left with the doctor.

Elizabeth's thought's turned to Michael. Where was he, he hadn't been to see her, maybe all that had happened to his family over the past few months had been to much for him, and Sharna's death was the last straw. She couldn't go to see him today, she would go tomorrow.

It was going to take a while to get to Manchester, so she rushed to get ready. Matthew had the carriage harnessed and ready which she was pleased about. She had no intention of asking James to join her. He would have to make his own way there.

The journey seemed long hot and dusty. The roads were dreadful, they had dried out after the winter and had deep ruts in them caused by the passage of wheels in wet weather. Eventually they arrived in Manchester and pulled up outside the lawyers offices. Elizabeth told Matthew he could go and get some nourishment in the nearest inn, which pleased him very much. She made her way up the stairs, she could hear voices, one of which she recognized as James's. How did he get here so fast she thought ! Of cause, he must have come last night and stayed in Manchester. He seemed very eager to know what her Fathers will contained. She took a deep breath and went in.

Richard Hyde sat behind his big oak desk, he had a wine glass in his hand which looked like whisky in it.

"Are Elizabeth," he said jumping up to greet her. "Thank you for coming, I hope the journey wasn't too unpleasant. Your cousin James and I where just having a drink and getting to know one another better. Please sit down".

Elizabeth mumbled something and sat in a leather chair opposite James. He was grinning at her, and seemed to have an air of arrogance about him. She could tell he had been drinking heavily.

"What do you think of my cousin Richard, isn't she a beauty, and she has spunk too. One would think twice about crossing her, she has very sharp claws".

Elizabeth felt his eyes on her, but she was determined that he wasn't going to get the better of her.

"I thought we were here to discuss my Father's will" she said looking at Richard Hyde.

"Of cause Elizabeth, and we will do that right now" he said getting up and walking over to a cabinet and taking out a large document that was tied with a blue ribbon, untying it he sat for a minute, before addressing Elizabeth.

"Your Father made this will out before he left for France, it was witnessed by myself and a colleague, it states that".

This is the last will and testament of William George Maybrey mill owner residing in the parish of Bardsley in the borough of Manchester, in the year of our lord eighteen thirty six. I hereby wish to declare that on my death, I leave to my daughter Elizabeth Charlotte Maybrey all my worldly goods which includes, Berkeley Grange and all adjoining lands and buildings on the said lands. Also I leave to her all businesses and investments which I own. I also leave her eight thousand pounds to help with the running of the above properties until such time as everything is settled.

To my nephew James Maybrey I leave the responsibility of running Bardsley mill, until my daughter Elizabeth marries. Then it must be returned to them both, so they can together secure the future of the mill and continue to help the people of Bardsley to prosper.

Richard Hyde took of his glasses and addressed Elizabeth.

"As you can see it was short and to the point. I think your Father thought he would be back home in a couple of months but that was not to be. I personally think it's a fair and well thought out will. And I am sure you will think the same when you have thought it over". Elizabeth clutched the arms of the chair until her knuckles went white. She wasn't going to give James the satisfaction of seeing her upset. She knew now by the expression on his face that this or something like it was going to happen. How stupid she had been, it was plain to everyone but her that a woman no matter what age, would never be allowed to take control of a cotton mill. She felt suddenly very vulnerable, and felt she had to get out of that office before she lost control of her feelings. It was no good fighting any more, no one was going to listen to what she had to say. She now knew how her Mother had felt living in a man's world; feeling trapped, and not allowed to make her own way in it, never to have her own opinions. Well she was determined it wasn't going to be like that for her. If she did ever get married she would pick someone like Michael who had respect for her and anything she had to say. Elizabeth thanked Richard Hyde for his kindness, and asked him to put the money her Father had left in a separate account in her name so she could access it when she wanted to. This he agreed to, and wished her luck for the future.

Elizabeth walked down the stairs to were Matthew was waiting. As the carriage was about to pull away James came to the window, and spoke to her.

"Elizabeth, it's no use fighting me on this; it's what your Father wanted. He expressed his hope to me that one day you and I would wed, and carry on the name of Maybrey".

"You lie" she said looking furious. "My Father would have discussed it with me before he would have mentioned it to you, and he did no such thing. I know what you're up to James, you're an opportunist, you saw a good opportunity here with my Father and you took it. I don't trust you, and I want you out of my house within the week, I own Berkeley Grange now, and there's nothing you can do about it" James grabbed her wrist.

"So you want to play dirty do you miss, you'll regret you ever crossed me. I'm used to getting my own way, and I'm hanged if a slip of a girl is going to get in my way". Elizabeth shouted to Matthew to get going, the carriage sprang forward and James stumbled back onto the pavement. Elizabeth settled back for the journey home happy in the knowledge that things weren't all going James's way. She thanked god that at least she had inherited some of her Father's strength to see this unfortunate business through to the end. It was good to be back home, she washed and changed into a clean gown, and feeling much better she went to ask Ada if anyone had called. Ada said it had been very quiet, there had been no visitors. She told Elizabeth that she had been to see the preacher and he had told her that the service for her Father was ten o'clock Sunday morning.

"Thank you Ada, I hope you will be there ? It will mean a lot to me".

"Of cause I'll be there miss we all will. And by the way miss the funeral for Sharna is taking place after your service is finished. Is it all right if we stay for it ?"

"Its quite all right Ada I'll be staying with you".

Elizabeth made her way to the church on Sunday morning for her Father's service. As the carriage pulled up out side the church she stepped down from it and felt a hand on her arm. It was James; he must have been waiting for her.

"Now don't make a fuss Elizabeth" he said guiding her to the church gate. "You and I will have to be seen together if only for appearances sake. When this is over you can go on your way".

"I have every intention of going my own way" she said defiantly, "As far away from you as is humanly possible".

The church yard was filled with people mostly businesses men who had been close to her Father. Elizabeth heard someone shout her name, turning round she saw Emily with her family. It was a relief to see them, she walked over to them.

"Thank you for coming, I was hoping you would be here today".

"It was the least we could do Elizabeth" said Mrs Arlington taking her hand. We thought a lot of your Father, and we are here today to express that". Emily gave here a big hug. "I'm so sorry Elizabeth I; don't know what to say to you. We can't imagine what you're going through at the moment".

"Thank you, you are all so kind, shall we go in, I think they are waiting for me to be seated first".

The service brought Elizabeth back to reality regarding her Father. She seemed to have put his death to the back of her mind. But now it was time to except that he wouldn't be coming back and she would never see him again. The tears came easily, and after the service she was surprisingly calm and relieved it was all over. Saying farewell to everyone she made her way into the graveyard to be with her Mother for a few minutes. As she was tidying the grave she heard her name being called, it was Michael; he stood with his back to the church wall and was beckoning her.

"Michael, thank goodness you're here, I was worried when I hadn't heard from you, are you all right?"

"Yes Elizabeth I'm fine I just came to see if you were ok after your Father's service".

"I'm fine Michael it was very hard for me but I'm glad it's over".

"I've had to stay with Pa today he's taking Sharna's death badly. Will you be going to the funeral; I wouldn't blame you if you felt you couldn't come after what you have been through today".

"You should have known I'd be there for you" she said taking his hands"

"I loved that little girl Elizabeth just as I"

"Love you" she said finishing his sentence.

"Yes, I'm not afraid to say it now, I love you Michael, you have been there for me whenever I've needed someone to talk too. At first it was only friendship, but you must have sensed there was something deeper". Suddenly she was in his arms his lips on hers and realising this wasn't a boy any longer but a man who loved her with a passion . She found herself responding to him enjoying the closeness and love they felt for one another. Releasing her with tears in his eyes he told her how much he loved her and hoped she felt the same. She didn't have to answer he knew by the look in her eyes that she felt the same. He took her face in his hands and kissed her gently on the lips.

"I didn't dare dream that you could feel this way" he said touching her cheek. "I've loved you for so long. I thought I'd go mad not being able to tell you. I know nothing can ever come of it, I just wanted to hear you say the words".

"What do you mean nothing can come of it, if we love one another it shouldn't matter what people think".

"Elizabeth, all I am at the moment is a stable hand; nobody will accept me into the company you keep. This will bring you disrespect from everyone".

"Yes, Michael some may have that attitude, you are right about that, but there are business men who started with nothing, and are now wealthy. There's nothing we can't do if we stick together. Don't abandon me now Michael when I need you most

"I will never do that" he said kissing her. "I still say we don't stand much of a chance, but if you're willing to be with me I suppose it's better to have tried than to give up".

"Oh, I'm so glad" she said taking his hand. "Come now let's say our farewell to Sharna, I'll help you through it. No one can touch us if we stay strong".

The whole town turned out for the funeral. They had filled the little church with spring flowers. Michael's family were very touched by it, and tried to thank everyone but there was just too many people. Elizabeth felt that her presence there had done some good in the eyes of the town's people. They all thanked her for coming, especially after having attended the service for her Father. After it was all over, Michael said he would see her later at the stables, as he would be able to come back to work now the funeral was over. She waved goodbye to him and walked to her carriage. As she went to step in she noticed James across the street, he was bending down from his horse talking to somebody, she couldn't make out who it was, hurriedly stepping into the carriage she told Matthew to return home.

 Michael made his way out through the side gate of the cemetery and along a path up to the main road. He decided to stay off the road and make his way along the river bank and through the woods up to Berkeley Grange. He was feeling really happy, remembering what had just occurred back at the church. Ten minutes later he had covered about half the distance through the woods when he heard a noise behind him, as he turned to look he felt something hit his head. The next thing he remembered was looking up and seeing two men standing over him. One had a piece of wood in his hand, and the other an iron bar, their faces were covered. One of the men grabbed his hair and said to him.

"What your about to get is a warning to stay away from Elizabeth Maybrey. If you don't heed this advice the next time we come to find you we won't be so lenient. Michael tried to get to his feet but couldn't make it. The blows rained down on him, he only remembered two then everything went black.

It was some time later that Elizabeth went to the stables to meet Michael and was surprised to find he wasn't there. She asked John if he'd seen him, he said no. She waited a little bit longer then started to get worried, she shouted to John to saddle the two horses and to follow her. It wasn't long before they found him; he was staggering up the hill on a path leading to the vegetable garden. Elizabeth dismounted and ran to him; he was in a bad way. Blood gushed from his head and one of his eyes looked black and swollen. In between tears she tried to reassure him he was going to be alright. They had quite a job to get him on to a horse, eventually succeeding. Finely they reached the manor John banged on the door until Mary opened it and helped them carry him to the kitchen. Ada got the shock of her life.

"Good Lord above ! What has happened, are you all right Miss Elizabeth ?"

"Yes Ada, it's not me that's hurt its Michael; it looks as if he's had some sort of accident".

"That's no accident miss" John said shaking his head. "He's been beaten up, and a bad beating at that".

"Beaten up" said Elizabeth looking shocked. "Who would do such a thing? He has never hurt a soul in his whole life".

"Well somebody had it in for him, by all account" Ada said looking distressed. She told Sarah to bring hot water and clean cloths to bath his wounds. Opening his clothing they saw large bruises on his body. Elizabeth told Mary to go to the east wing and open up the old nursery and to light a fire in there.

"The old nursery miss why that's not been opened for years" she said looking puzzled.

"I know it hasn't, I have my reasons for doing this Mary now go! Take fresh bedding and warm the bed with a warming pan". Elizabeth turned to Ada.

"No one will think of looking there for him".

"Do you think whoever done this will come looking for him again then miss".

"I don't know Ada I'm not taking any chances. At least he'll be safe there".

Elizabeth told everyone not to say a word on what had occurred, she knew they were all loyal and would say nothing. Soon they had him settled in bed; he fell fast asleep for about three hours. Elizabeth sat by his side for most of that time. When he woke he opened his eyes and said. "How long have you been there Elizabeth"?

"Not to long, are you feeling any better?"

"I'm ok, just a bit sore. You haven't told my Father about this have you ? He can't take any more shocks".

"No of cause I haven't, you must stay here till your well; he won't miss you for a while yet. You don't have to say anything about what happened to you until your better".

"It makes no difference if I tell you now or later" he said trying to sit up. " I was deep in thought and didn't hear them coming, I didn't stand much of a chance, there were two of them, one had an iron bar. I was told if I didn't stop seeing you they would be back".

"Who were these men, did you recognise them ?"

"Oh yes, just the one, he had something over his face but I got a glimpse of his forearm, he has a tattoo of an eagle I've seen it before. I delivered some things to the Apprentice House once, it was there I noticed his arm, it was Scarsfield all right I'd know that tattoo anywhere".

"And I know who put him up to it" Elizabeth said looking so angry she could hardly speak. "It was James, who else could it have been. I should have told you before but you had so many things on your mind I didn't want to add to your troubles. He's been asking me to marry him so he can get his hands on the business, there's know other explanation. He's been playing on the fact that I would have difficulty running the mill. I know he's right about the mill but I would rather sell it than marry someone like him".

Michael shook his head.

"This man could be a danger to you Elizabeth, if he finds he's getting nowhere with you, he may think of other ways to get his hands on your estate".

"Like what" she said looking puzzled

"Just try to think how he thinks. You are the heir to this estate; if you were removed he would be next in line to inherit".

"By removed you mean he would try to get rid of me. How ? An accident perhaps".

"Elizabeth, I didn't mean to frighten you, but I think he's been behind all that's been happening around this house ever since he got here".

"Does this mean he had something to do with Sharna's death? Oh ! Michael no, you don't think he killed her do you".

"No, not directly, but I think he dishonoured her and she killed herself".

"Oh, I hope you are wrong about this, if only she could tell us what really happened". Michael thought for a minute then sat up quickly.

"Wait a minute maybe there is a way she can tell us".

"For goodness sake Michael how on earth could she do that ?"

"By her diary of cause, why didn't I think of it before? I told you she was a good scholar she wrote constantly, every night she would write in her diary what she had done that day".

"You think she might have written something in it until the day she died ?"

"I'm sure of it Elizabeth I watched her every day she never missed"

"Where would it be now do you think ? If we can get some kind of evidence against James it will give us something to fight back with".

"Are you really ready to face something like this right now Michael you aren't well, let's wait until you are feeling better"?

"No Elizabeth we have waited to long now, if you don't start fighting back this man will end up owning everything your Father has worked for all these years".

"Your right of cause, I'll see what I can find, you have a rest, I'll send Sarah up with some food for you ".

Elizabeth gave instructions to Sarah to prepare a plate of food for Michael, and to take it to him, making sure there was nobody around. Ten she asked Mary to follow her upstairs. They passed James apartments Elizabeth asked her if she had seen him.

"Yes miss he called earlier when you were out. He said he would be back around seven o'clock to collect some things".

"What things ? Did he say ".

"No miss, that's all he said".

"All right Mary, I've brought you up here to help me search Sharna's room. I believe she had a diary do you know anything about it ?".

"Oh yes she was always writing in it".

"When was the last time you saw her with it?"

"Oh let me think, Ah ! Yes that would be when she was last with us in her old room, before she had to go to Mr and Mrs Maybrey's apartments. Is it very important we find this diary?"

"Yes Mary, I think her Father would want it back so I decided to look for it" Elizabeth wasn't going to tell her the real reason.

They entered the little girl's room and looked around. There was very little in there just a bed wash stand and cupboards.

"You strip the bed Mary and I'll check the cupboards. The only thing she found in one of them was a change of clothes. As she pushed them aside there was something underneath that surprised Elizabeth. She found two geography books from the library. It was obvious that Sharna was borrowing them to read at night when she had finished her work. This girl was no thief; she had a longing to learn about the world outside her little room. Suddenly the room felt icy cold, Elizabeth shivered. Finding nothing in the room she told Mary to go and help Ada with the evening meal, making the excuse she would look again later.

Elizabeth looked in on Michael to see if he was all right, he was asleep so she went to get changed for dinner.

Sitting in the dinning room alone, her food untouched she sat and watched the flames in the fireplace lap around the wooden logs. She remembered how she used to sit in the evenings with her Mamma, talking about what they had done that day, and making plans for the future. She never missed her as much as she did at this moment. Wiping away a tear she was about to get up when the door burst open. James walked in and greeted Elizabeth as if nothing had passed between them.

"Elizabeth, have you finished dinner already ? I'm famished, haven't had a thing all day" She got up to leave but he closed the door

"Please don't go we have things to discuss".

"You and I have nothing to discuss" she said feeling her face reddening , but one thing only. Why did you send two thugs to beat Michael up ? It's no use you denying it, I know it was you".

"Really Elizabeth don't you think I would have better things to do with my time than to get involved with people like that. I don't understand for one minute why you interact with any of the town's people. You shouldn't even be speaking to them".

"I saw you, talking to them the day of the service" said Elizabeth defiantly. "And I've also seen you talking to that man from the Apprentice House. I know he was one of the men that attacked Michael".

James went quiet and poured some tea into a cup, he didn't look up. "And how may I ask could you know that ?

"Never mind how I know. This Scarsfield person will be sorry he ever laid a finger on him".

"You really are obsessed with your little stable hand aren't you Elizabeth. There's no future for you and him you know, you'll be laughed out of town. Just think how the local paper will read. Heiress marries stable hand; your Father would turn in his grave".

"Leave my Father out of this. You are just jealous because I've found someone who I enjoy being with. I have a feeling James that you have never been close to anyone in your life, is that not true ? Elizabeth noticed she somehow had hit a nerve by the expression on his face.

"Yes I suppose your right in a way; I've never had feelings for anyone until I meet you Elizabeth. I know you don't believe me, but it's true. I've done a lot of things in my life that I haven't been proud of, but I also told you once that I was willing to change. Things haven't always been easy for me. I've had to fight all my life to hang on to my place in society. I thought to take what you wanted was the only way to succeed. But since I've meet you I see life can be quite different, and I'm willing to make that change if you'll have me. I'll be anything you want me to be".

"James I have a feeling you mean what you say in your own way, but two wrongs don't make a right. None of us can help what we are; you just can't change your personality over night. And I wouldn't want anyone who wasn't their true self. I told you before of my decision and I stand by it. I'm sorry if you don't like it but that's the way it is".

"And that's your final decision is it" he said his eyes blazing, "You my change your mind if you find out it's the only way to keep the mill". Elizabeth walked to the door turning she said. "I think it's best if you find somewhere else to live James, it will make things easier for us all".

"You don't have to worry " he said sarcastically, "I've already rented a house in town I move in tomorrow".

Elizabeth gave a sigh of relief and closed the door. Feeling completely exhausted she went to say goodnight to Michael. Then retired to bed. It had been a day she wanted to forget; asleep she would be able to forget everything at least for a few hours.

****

CHAPTER TEN
THE DIARY
****

Elizabeth must have been asleep about four hours when she was woken by someone calling her name. Sitting up she stretched over and lit a candle. The room was very dark except for a pale light coming in from the window; she thought maybe she had been dreaming. Getting out of bed she unlocked the door, thinking she had better go and see if Michael was all right. She wasn't to happy about leaving her room but it had to be done. The candle light danced along the walls and ceilings as she walked along the corridors. Her heart was pounding in her chest; she told herself how silly she was to be scared in her own home. Reaching the nursery she peeped in, he was fast asleep, better leave him to rest she thought closing the door. As she walked back to her room she was about to go in when she heard her name being called again. It didn't make any sense that somebody would be roaming around in the middle of the night. Turning she walked back along the landing deciding to make her way to the servants quarters, things seemed quiet enough there. Again she turned and walked past James's apartments, she knew he wasn't there as she had seen him riding away from the house earlier. She was about to go back to her room when she noticed Sharna's door to her room was open. I'm sure I shut it earlier she thought ! Looking in, everything was as she had left it. Walking to the window she looked out across the garden, it was to dark to see anything. Elizabeth shivered wondering why it was always so cold in this room, the rest of the house was definitely much warmer. Turning to go back to her room she stepped on one of the floor boards it creaked loudly under her weight. Looking down she noticed the board was very loose Putting the candle down she lifted it up and found there was something inside. Reaching in she pulled out a little brown book with a clasp on one side, undoing the clasp she opened it and read what was on the inside cover.

To our granddaughter Sharna on her thirteenth birthday

All our love Grandma and Grandad 1836

Elizabeth closed the book quickly, and made her way back to her room. It had been under their very noses all this time, she thought ! Shaking her head and locking her bedroom door she put the book under her pillow and climbed into bed, it would have to wait till morning she was so tired.

To everyone's surprise Michael was up and back in the stables with John the next day. He didn't look to good but insisted he was all right and wanted to get back to work. Elizabeth sent him a message to meet her down by the river at ten o'clock. She was a little early so she sat under the willow tree in the shade. Spring was well on its way, everywhere looked fresh and green after the winter, and the river had slowed to a steady flow. She tried what had happened to Sharna to the back of her mind, but it wasn't easy. She kept thinking of the night she had died, and how she had begged her to take her back to her old room. Elizabeth just hadn't known how upset she had been. If only I had helped her she thought ! Wiping tears from her eyes she looked down at the little book in her hands, she went to open it but couldn't for fear of what she would find. In a little while Michael came over the hill, he wasn't his usual self but she didn't expect him to be happy after what had happened to him. Elizabeth asked him if he was alright, he just nodded and sat down.

"The book you told me about Michael, Sharna's well I've found it" she said handing it to him. "I haven't read it, I think she would have wanted you to read it, I know how she loved you so".

He opened it, there were many pages given over to everyday happenings. Coming over on the boat from Ireland, how they were all very sick, because of the weather. Then settling in to their new home in Bardsley. And how she was surprised to find how similar the countryside was to Ireland. Going quickly through the rest of the pages he came to the last entry in the book. April 26th

This is the last time I will put my thoughts into words. There is no way out for me now my family are in danger. I have dishonoured them in the worst possible way. I must be very wicked to have attracted the devils servant like I have. Time is short there is only one way left to me, may God have Mercy on my soul.

Michael handed the book to Elizabeth, he couldn't read anymore. On reading it her heart sank.

"Oh Michael, I'm so sorry, it looks as if you were right, he was treating her like he treated those slaves who worked on the plantation. The man must have thought he was still in Jamaica. How could he do such a wicked thing, to an innocent girl"?

Michael jumped to his feet throwing his arms in the air.

"I'll kill him the swine, he not only dishonoured my sister but he must have been threatening to kill her family if she spoke up. Well it's going to be his turn to be terrified when I meet up with him".

"Michael this man has standing in the community, if you attack him it's you that will be put in jail not him. Do you really want him to walk away from all this unscathed ?"

"But what else can I do, this is the only way I know of fighting back"

"No, your wrong Michael there is a better way of doing it, you must listen to me. We will go to the police, they have to listen to me, I have friends with a lot of influence in the community who will help us".

"I know it makes sense Elizabeth, it's just that I feel so helpless".

"I know dear" she said putting her arms around his waist "But we must do this the right way ".

"All right I'll try it, but if it doesn't work, then I do it my way. What ever happens he's a dead man". Elizabeth had never seen Michael like this before, the furious look on his face frightened her. For just a split second he looked much older than his seventeen years. He needed to vent his anger on someone, and she knew just the person. She took his hand and started to climb the bank.

"Come, I want you to saddle the horses, we have to make a little visit to the Apprentice house". He was just about to ask why; when he read her thought's smiling broadly he nodded grasping what she meant.

Instead of riding along the main roads they rode over Hawks Peak and down a steep incline to the east of the town and into the lane leading to the Apprentice House. Tying the horses up they walked through the vegetable garden. Elizabeth banged on the door, after a while they heard a shuffling as someone came down the hall. Scarsfield's wife opened the door, as she recognised Elizabeth she turned and tried to go back down the hall, but Elizabeth caught her arm.

"Not so quick madam, Where is your husband, I wish to speak to him". The woman pointed down the hallway then disappeared into the kitchen. They found him stretch out in the front parlour in front of the fire asleep, the smell of alcohol filled the room. Michael stepped forward and kicked the stool from under his feet. His great body lunged forward and landed on the floor. Opening his eyes he stirred up at them, trying to focus. "What the hell ! He said struggling to his feet. Michael grabbed his coat and pulled him up.

"Get up, you poor excuse for a man" said Elizabeth shaking her finger at him, "Did you think that you could get away with beating one of my workers half to death. Confess now and perhaps I'll be lenient with you". Scarsfield looked from one to the other, with a look of fear on his face.

"I don't know what you're talking about" he said red in the face. "You don't know it was me what done it".

"We know because you never covered your arms, Michael saw the tattoo you have on your arm as you were hitting him, so don't deny it".

"Lots of people have tattoo's doesn't mean it was me" he said looking indignant. Elizabeth was getting quite angry at this point. "Are you denying it then, answer me, you poor excuse for a man" Scarsfield said nothing

"Very well, you leave me no choice; you and your wife will leave this place and never return. You have two hours to get out, if you are not gone by then the police will be informed and you will be charged with assault. I will also make enquires into how you have been running the Apprentice House. I think we will be able to obtain enough evidence from the children alone to jail you for a long time".
Scarsfield's face suddenly got very red indeed, he took a step towards Elizabeth but

Michael came between them.

"You can't do that" he said trying desperately trying to think of a way out. "I work for James Maybrey I take my orders from him". Elizabeth pushed Michael aside.

"I don't know who told you that, James Maybrey has control of Berkeley Mill and that is all he has control of. I am mistress of Berkeley Grange, including the land and all buildings on that land. And this includes the Apprentice House, so be warned, "YOU WILL ! Be gone when I say, or you will take the consequences". Elizabeth turned and walked quickly down the hall. She waited for Michael outside who followed a minute later. She asked him what he had said to Scarsfield after she left. But he wouldn't tell her. "Let's just say, you can be sure he won't still be here in two hours". Elizabeth took a deep breath.

"I'm so glad you were with me today, I don't know if I could have done this alone".

"Are you kidding" he said grinning, "You were great the way you stood up to him. No man could have done better".

"Do you really think so" she said looking pleased with herself.

"Well that's one person who won't be bothering us again" he said helping her on to her horse.

"Good heavens I've just thought of something Michael. The children ! Who's going to look after them now? I was to busy trying to get rid of those people I forgot who would replace them. Do you know anyone ?"

"Let me think, Mrs Cross is out ! She has enough to do in the soup kitchen. The only person I can think of is Pa, he's great with kids and Luke is old enough to help now".

"Are they still working in the mill ?"

"Yes but they are down to three days between them, I didn't tell you, you had so many things on your mind"

"Michael, why didn't you mention it, I could have helped you out. They wouldn't have had enough money to feed themselves. Tonight I want you to come back here, and check if those people have gone. If all's clear move your family in as soon as you can. Once all this business with the mill has been completed I'll get a woman as house keeper to look after things to help your Father. The boys will be all right, but the girls need a woman to look after them".

"I don't know how to thank you Elizabeth, You've done so much for us all ready".

"You don't have to thank me; your Father will find it quite hard looking after all those children. He will earn every penny he gets. And don't worry about their jobs at the mill; I'll inform Mr Smithfield of the situation. And I'll tell him not to say anything to anyone. I'm pretty certain they won't be missed if they were only working a few days. Now let's get back I have a lot to think about, and people to see in the next few days. It's about time I started fighting back. I want to hold on to Berkeley Grange and the business far more than James who is out to take it from me" Michael grabbed Elizabeth's reins and stopped her horse.

"Elizabeth you have to promise me you won't put yourself in danger, where ever you go in the next day or two I want to go with you" he said looking worried.

"Well if you insist Michael, I can't think of a reason why you can't go with me. I would have to get you some clothes though, you can't go around with a lady in rags can you" she said smiling.

"Lady is it" he said grinning, "Well lets see how good the lady is at riding, I bet I can beat you back home" he swung himself into the saddle hit his boot with his whip and away he went. The ride was exhilarating and Elizabeth felt like a new person when she reached the stables, the air seemed to have cleared her head, Michael was well back before her of cause she could never beat him at riding. She told him to come over to the manor later and she would find him the clothes she had promised him. As she arrived back Mary was coming out of the dinning room.

"Oh there you are miss, a messenger called about a half an hour ago he left a letter. I've put it in the drawing room".

"Why thank you Mary I'll read it right away, how is everything in the kitchen are you managing all right ?"

"Yes thank you miss".

"Tell cook I'll be there soon".

"Yes miss"

The letter was from Samuel, he apologised for not coming to see her but said he would call later that evening and hoped she would be home. Elizabeth was so thankful he was coming to visit her she felt so safe when he was around, he seemed to have a calming effect on her. As a child she saw more of him than her Father who was always busy at the mill. She used to resent her Father for never being there for her but as she got older she realised the reason for his absence, he had so many responsibilities, she just wished he could have shared with her something of his life and talked to her about the mill. Now it was too late, she would have to find her own way in the world and maybe it would be a good thing after all, this way she would be much stronger. She threw the letter into the fire and made her way to the kitchen.

Two hours later Michael arrived, Elizabeth had found some worn but good clothes of her Fathers to give him, they were a little big but would do, they consisted of a brown woollen jacket and jodhpurs and a pair of black riding boots. After he had put them on Elizabeth couldn't believe how different he looked, she thought him very handsome but didn't tell him so.

Later that evening Elizabeth waited patiently for Samuel to arrive. It wasn't long before she heard his carriage pull up in the driveway; she went quickly to open the door for him. As he stepped from the carriage she through her arms around him.

"Good heavens ! What's this, he said surprised at the attention "Have I really been away that long".

"Oh Samuel, I've missed you so, you must promise never to stay away this long again"

"I have a feeling it's not just my absence you are upset about my dear, come inside and tell me how you have been coping since my last visit" Elizabeth ordered some tea and when it arrived they sat around the fire in the drawing room, it tended to get a little cold in the evenings even in spring. After a while Elizabeth found herself talking for what must have been a good ten minutes. She went through all that had happened since her Mamma had died. Samuel listened patiently as she spoke, when she had finished he sat there for a minute saying nothing, then said.

"You know Elizabeth you will have to be careful what you accuse this man of. If you haven't got definite proof of his miss deeds then you could find yourself in more trouble than him"

"But surely Samuel the diary will be proof enough"

"Are, but is it proof, the child doesn't mention him by name, I'm no lawyer but even I can see that this evidence will be thrown out of court". Elizabeth stared wide eyed at him.

"What you're saying is I would be a fool going to the police about this, that they wouldn't even listen to me".

"I'm afraid that's it my dear".

"Oh Samuel I was hoping this would be the turning point for me, that he would be brought to court and be put away for a long time. But I can see I've been deluding myself, he's won again hasn't he ?"

"Well not necessarily, I've been making a few inquires of my own about James Maybrey because I felt it my duty to your Father, and I must say I wasn't overly impressed on what I've heard"

"Really" said Elizabeth "What kind of things ?"

"Well it seems he's been gambling and loosing heavily, he has i,o,u's all over the place, and some of these people are out for blood. And there is something else, it's only a rumour but there is a ship that's just arrived from Jamaica it's docked in Liverpool. The captain of that ship has been causing quite a stare, saying he has some information for the police about a certain person in the community. We don't exactly know what it's about because he was very drunk at the time he was making these accusations".

"You don't think they have tracked him down for whatever he did there do you ? How did you find out about this"?

"Remember the shipping company I went to see about your Father, well I have a lot of friends there. This sea captain mentioned James Maybrey by name saying he had something to tell the police about . Things like this get around very fast in this town. I can't guarantee what I've told you is true, we will have to see".

"Well what if I go to the police and just tell them of my suspicions ? Elizabeth said looking excited. " Then I would be in the right place to find out if they know anything".

"Well that's up to you Elizabeth although I think you will be wasting your time. Do you want me to do anything for you ? Like making any more enquires about him".

"I can't think of anything at the moment Samuel, I was thinking of going to see Richard Hyde this week. Do you think you could come with me, he may be able to give me some advice?"

"Of cause dear child, what day do you want me to be here ?".

"I think the day after tomorrow, will that be all right with you ?"

"Yes that will be fine, I'm here for another reason too, I wanted to give you this. Samuel took out a pouch from his pocket and gave it to her. Looking puzzled Elizabeth tipped the contents on to her hand. She was surprised to see the necklace she had given him to sell to start the soup kitchen.

"I don't understand why you are still in possession of my necklace?"

"Well I knew how much you loved it, and I remember your Mamma wearing it on her wedding day. She was as beautiful as you are now. So I decided you must have it back".

Elizabeth ran her fingers over the glistening stones as tears ran down her cheeks.

"But I don't understand where did the money come from to pay for the soup kitchen , It cost a fortune to set up".

"Now don't you worry about that, I may be only a retired school master but I am rich in my own right. My parents were very wealthy, I'm sure in the past I've told you about them. They had a sugar plantation in America. When I was fourteen they sent me to England to finish my education. I never returned to America, I wanted to become a teacher in England so my brother inherited the business. Then five years ago he died and left me quite a bit of money. So you see you don't have to worry, I never even missed the money that it cost to pay for it".

"I can never repay you for what you have done this day Samuel you are a true friend, I feel truly blessed to have known you" She kissed him on the cheek .

"Now now, you'll have a grown man weeping in a minute" he said wiping his eyes. Elizabeth sat back in her chair and took a long look at this ageing old man, with his sparkling black eyes and snowy white hair and beard. Suddenly a thought came into her head, and she didn't know how she hadn't thought of it before. He had been in love with her Mamma all these years and kept it a secret. She was surprised to find herself saying ! "You loved her didn't you Samuel, Mamma, you loved her all these years. Did you never tell her so ? He looked very startled; leaving his chair he stood in front of the fireplace "It was that obvious was it ? He said turning to look at her".

"No I assure you it never occurred to me till this very moment Samuel. Do you think you could bring yourself to tell me about it"?

"Well there's nothing much to tell really, I started to call on your Mamma before she met your Father. Things were going well for us so I asked her to marry me, she said yes so I called on her Father to ask permission for us to marry. He turned me down, seems a teacher wasn't quite good enough for their daughter. As you already know your Mamma's family were very well to do. I begged them for their consent but they wouldn't change their minds and that's about it really".

"And you never married Samuel, was it because of Mamma or didn't you meet anyone you felt you could share your life with ?"

"Oh I don't know really, I suppose I didn't put enough effort into finding someone else, my work took over my life and I haven't regretted it. I've loved every minute of my teaching career".

"And your pupils have loved you to Samuel, for I know it's not just the rich children you have taught".

"Thank you dear that's very kind, now I must be on my way it' getting late, I've enjoyed our little talk. And I hope you will be careful how you go about this business with James Maybrey. The only way you are going to get rid of him is if you play him at his own game. I'll be here the day after tomorrow, I'll come early it will take us a while to get to Manchester".

"Thank you Samuel, I'll just ring for Mathew to bring your carriage around".

The next day Elizabeth and Michael went to see the police. They listened patiently to what she had to say, then explained to her there was nothing they could do about the situation as there was no proof against James. Sharna's diary didn't mention anyone by name. All they could do was interview him and ask him a few questions, but they thought it would be just a formality. If they hadn't any more proof than this diary then they couldn't help them. Elizabeth asked if James Maybrey's name had come to their attention in the passed week or so, but they had heard nothing about him.

It was of cause what Elizabeth had expected. She asked them to keep in touch with her if they heard anything, they said they would so she thanked them and left. Michael was very quiet on the way home.

"Your very quiet Michael is there anything wrong?"

"I think we are kidding ourselves if we think we can bring this man to Justice Elizabeth. I think the best thing is to forget it. I could be making trouble for my family. If I'm put in jail because of this, my family will suffer. Elizabeth thought for a minute.

"You are right of cause; it was selfish of me to involve you in all of this. From now on I'll see to everything myself, I know how hard all of this must have been for you".

"You do understand then, about my family I mean ?"

"Of cause I do, and I love you for it, your first priority must be towards your Father and those children. Don't look so down hearted were not finished yet, I don't give up that easy".

Samuel came to Berkeley Grange on the day he had promised to travel to

Manchester with Elizabeth. Richard Hyde greeted them warmly as they entered his office. Samuel apologised for not letting him know they wished to speak to him, and hoped they wouldn't take up to much of his time. "I assure you Samuel you and Elizabeth are welcome to see me anytime. I always make time for friends such as you. Now what brings you here this fine day ?".

They both explained in their own way why they had come. Elizabeth telling him in no uncertain terms on what had occurred in the last few months.

"Have you been to the police about Maybrey" Mr Hyde said looking surprised.

"Yes, said Elizabeth, I went to see them yesterday they told us we didn't have enough evidence to charge him".

"Well, with what you have told me I'd say they were correct. The only advice that I can give you is to wait until he eventually breaks the law. And by what I have observed it won't be very long".

"Does that mean you have had dealings with him recently" asked Elizabeth looking hopeful

"As a matter of fact he was in this very office yesterday morning in a very agitated state. He wanted me to represent him in court next week. But I explained I couldn't take on another case as I was to busy. A certain person who I can't name is suing him for none payment of a debt. I gave him the name of another lawyer and explained there wasn't much hope of him winning the case as the other person had a signed I.o.u. My advice to him was to pay what he owed, and walk away. It was then he admitted the money owed was a very substantial amount and he couldn't pay it".

"I knew it" said Elizabeth throwing her arms in the air. "He's been using every penny from my Fathers business to gamble with".

"This could be a big problem for her if it carries on" said Samuel, at least until she marries".

"Look" said Mr Hyde, "My advice to you both is to wait a little bit longer, and I somehow feel as if our Mr James Maybrey is going to dig his own grave pretty soon. Let's see what happens at the court hearing. He's not going anywhere because there is too much at stake. He won't relinquish his hold on the mill, I fancy he likes the power of being in charge. So he's going to hold on to it as long as he can".

"I'm scared in case we have to go bankrupt and have to close down" said Elizabeth. "It will mean all those people at the mill will lose their jobs. Half of them will die of starvation; they are in a bad way now".

"I understand my dear" he said, and I know how you feel about the mill and its people, but we have to keep our heads about this. I will do all I can to help you in this matter but you must be patient".

"I'm sorry of cause your right" Elizabeth said standing up. "We will leave it in your hands, and thank you, you have been so understanding". Elizabeth left feeling as if at last she wasn't entirely alone, it was a good feeling.

After church on Sunday Elizabeth and Michael called at the Apprentice House to see how his Father was managing after his move. As they walked through the gate they had quite a surprise. They were meet by the sound of children laughing loudly and enjoying themselves immensely. At least ten of them were planting vegetable seeds with Michaels Father. It was nice to here them so happy, Elizabeth could only guess how they must have suffered living with those awful people. He told them there was no sign of Scarsfield and this wife they had left for good. They both stayed for about half an hour to get an idea on what Michael's Father needed for the children then said goodbye and left.

When they arrived back they decided to go for a ride and have lunch out so Michael went into the stables to saddle the horses while Elizabeth walked back to the manor. As she reached the end of the path James came round the corner on horse back skidding to a halt his horse tried to avoid her, she stumbled and feel to the ground. He jumped from his horse and pulled her to her feet, brushing her gown down she flew at him and shouted, "What do you think your doing you nearly killed me

"I wish I had you little witch" he said with such hate in his eyes. What's the idea of you going to the police about me saying I killed that servant?"

"I didn't say you killed her directly, but you might well have done for all I know. She was just a child for god's sake, and you dishonoured her. She wasn't one of your Jamaican slaves she was a highly intelligent and sensitive girl who would have done well for herself in this world until you came along and destroyed her life".

"Rubbish she was nothing ! He said his eyes blazing, "I can get a thousand like her any day of the week".

"I don't want to listen to this" she said opening the gate to the rose garden. "I want you to go; you're not fit to be in my presence". James rushed at her and pushed her through the gate. "I'll teach you whose master here" he said pinning her against the hedge. He started to tear at her cloths, she managed to grab his hand and bit it as hard as she could. He let go for a second yelling with pain, seizing her chance she ran back through the gate and headed for the stables. Running up the path she ran straight into Michael who was bringing the horses to the Manor. He saw at once how distressed she was and how her cloths were torn. He dropped the reins and ran passed her, she tried to stop him yelling Michael, NO ! It's just what he wants". She was too late, he launched himself at James who had retrieved his whip from the ground, raising it he tried to hit him but Michael grabbed his arm and the pair of them fell to the ground. They rolled over and over ending up under James's horse. Michael grabbed the stirrup and pulled himself up. James got to his feet and hit him in the face, he staggered back for a moment shaking his head. Elizabeth ran forward and held Michael's arm.

"Please stop it, Please !. He didn't seem to hear her; he pulled her arm away and went for James with what seemed to be the strength of six men. He administered three blows which sent him crashing to the ground. James lay quite still. Michael stood over him and said to him.

"Only for Elizabeth you would be dead now, you can thank her for your life. Stepping over him he led the horses to the main door of the manor and tied them up Elizabeth followed him. The incident had shaken them up quite a bit so they decided to go to Hawks Peak to be on their own for a bit. Sitting in their usual place they went over the mornings events Michael put his arm around Elizabeth and kissed her cheek.

"I'm so sorry Elizabeth I just couldn't help myself back there. The thought of him touching you nearly drove me crazy; I don't know how I didn't kill him".

"In my heart I knew you couldn't have done it Michael. You are different from him, you are honourable and he isn't. I understand why you did what you did, but I'm worried what James will do now. He will definitely go to the police and try to get you arrested; you are not safe here now"

"I suppose your right, what do you think I should do, I'm so sorry Elizabeth this is all my fault"

"Don't you worry" she said patting his hand. "I know just the place to hide you, when they come to the house. We will have to go back soon he could have gone to the police already".

When they got back she took him into the library. Walking to the book case she removed a couple of books and touched a tiny lever at the back. To Michael's surprise the whole bookcase swung out and revealed a tiny room. There was a very small table in there with a lamp on it and a chair. Elizabeth laughed at the look on his face.

"It's all right, it's a priest hole, it was incorporated into the manor when it was built. You'll have plenty of time to hide if anyone comes, it will mean you will have to stay here for a while".

"Hiding me like this could cause you a lot of trouble Elizabeth are you sure about this?

"Yes I'm quite sure, we promised to face this together didn't we. Come now I have to speak to Ada and the girls, they will have to know what's happening".

Elizabeth made everyone swear not to reveal the hiding place, and reassured them all that no harm would befall them for keeping silent.

It wasn't long before the police arrived to question everyone. Elizabeth explained that she hadn't seen Michael for two hours. She tried to explain about what happened but all they seemed to want to do was arrest him. They asked if they could search the house and grounds, telling them they could go anywhere they liked she took herself off to the kitchen to be with the servants in case they were asked any questions. Ada was doing all she could to stop Sarah from shaking so much. The child was obviously very frightened. Elizabeth pushed her into the pantry and told her to tidy all the shelves, and not to come out. The police did question the servants without noticing Sarah hiding in the pantry but got no information out of them. They begged her pardon for the intrusion then left.

****

CHAPTER ELEVEN
THE COURT HEARING
****

Elizabeth kept Michael hidden at Berkeley Grange until the day of the court hearing against James for none payment of debt. It was to be heard at the Court of Passage in Manchester. Circuit judges usually sat four times a year, but as there where no judges in the area at this particular time, the Mayor of Manchester was to preside over the court, as he was also a justice of the peace. It wasn't hard to gather this information as gossip seemed to be a favourite pastime for the people of Bardsley.

They both set out at seven in the morning giving them plenty of time to get there. The journey was very pleasant; summer was well on its way. Fresh emerald green fields stretched out as far as the eye could see. And the hedge rows were full of wild roses, and sweet smelling herbs. Michael almost admitted that England's countryside matched that of Ireland. He told Elizabeth that one day he would take her to the little village where he had been born.

"Can you describe it to me " she said, "I would love to see it".

"Well, it's only a tiny village; it's called Balingarry just west of Kilkenny southern Ireland. It's so beautiful there, with its white washed cottages and rolling hills".

"You miss it very much don't you Michael ?"

"Yes, I suppose I do a little, it seems a million miles away to me now. But I don't regret it for one minute. I have the love of the most beautiful girl in the world" he said kissing her, "There is no one on this earth who is as happy as I am at this moment".

"That is so sweet" she said kissing him back and laying her head on his shoulder. The rest of the journey past quite quickly. There was an hour to spare when they arrived so she told Matthew to find out exactly were the court was while they went for something to eat in one of the local taverns. Twenty minutes later Matthew arrived to say he'd located the court and he thought it would take them about five minutes to get there. Elizabeth had to reassure Michael on entering the court house, as he seemed very nervous, she couldn't blame him, it was a very intimidating place. A large stone building stood before them with steps leading up to round marble columns at the top. The entrance being enormous oak doors, which opened into a very large foyer. Stairs meandered both side of the room up to the next floor. And above that was a large stained glass dome which cascaded coloured light down to the floor below. Elizabeth thought the building very beautiful and would have liked to have looked around, but at the moment they had other things on their mind. They eventually found the main court room. The judge's bench was directly opposite them as they walked in. The prisoners dock to the left of that. Galleries over looked the room on both sides, while oak panelling filled every wall. The seating was composed of long benches on different levels, sloping down to the centre were two tables finished off the picture. They made their way along to the right and sat in the middle of the top bench, not wanting to be on full view, as the court got under way it wasn't long before the room filled up with people of every description. The galleries above seating locals who seemed to think it was a day out for them. The noise got to be quite deafening, suddenly in amongst the people she spotted Samuel's sister, why was she here, it was very strange. She saw Elizabeth and made her way over to them.

"Anna, what are you doing here" Elizabeth said looking puzzled, is Samuel with you?

"No my dear not yet at any rate, he told me to tell you not to move from the court until he arrives. I can't tell you anymore as I am as much in the dark as you are".

"How very strange Anna, Oh, well we had just better stay here until he arrives then".

"Do you know much about these allegations against your cousin" asked Anna "Samuel tells me this person whoever it is has brought him to court because he owes him a substantial amount of money. Is that correct ?"

"I'm afraid I only know what you do, there's one thing I cannot understand though is why he would put himself in this position. I mean to humiliate himself in court like this it doesn't make sense".

"Maybe he thinks by attending a court in Manchester no one will know about it".
"Well I hope he knows what he's doing because it will be in the papers tomorrow" Elizabeth said shaking her head,. Michael pointed to the door at the front of the court saying.

"I think it's about to start".

The door opened and the judge entered, everyone stood up in respect. He wore a long dark blue cassock with a hood; he seemed to be about sixty years of age. There was no expression at all on his bearded face as he took his seat. He banged a gavel very loudly on the bench and called for order; everyone went quiet and sat down. He ordered that James Maybrey be brought into court. A minute later they brought James from below the prisoners dock up some stairs, he looked surprisingly relaxed. Nodding to his lawyer he climbed into the dock and was sworn in giving his name and address. The judge addressed him.

"James Maybrey you have been brought here today because of a debt you won't or cannot pay to a certain business man whose name I have decided to keep anonymous. Do you plead guilty or not guilty" Before he could answer his lawyer stood up and spoke.

"My lord, before my client answers I wish to dismiss the allegations on the grounds that their isn't a case to answer. The Judge looked a bit irritated.

"What do you mean sir, there's no case to answer".

"Well my lord, it's been drawn to my attention only yesterday that the person who has brought these allegations against my client has had an unfortunate accident in his home. Apparently he was found dead at the bottom of his cellar steps with a broken neck" There was a sudden out burst from the gallery, which the judge had to silence. "Anymore out burst's like that again and you will all be thrown out" he said banging his gavel on the bench. "I won't stand any noise in my court room" They all went silent, the lawyer went on.

"I've spoken to the police, they say it was a clear accident, he must have slipped on some oil that had been spilt on the next to top stair. His family say he wasn't a well man before this happened. We are all sorry for their loss, as I'm sure my lord will reiterate". The Judge spoke to James.

"Well James Maybrey it seems you have avoided the full arm of the law this time. As you have good standing in the community I have no option but to dismiss the case against you. The Judge was about to say something else when the door at the back of the court was flung open and in came a policeman with two men. To Elizabeth's astonishment she recognised one as Samuel, the other man she didn't know who seemed decidedly unsteady on his feet. Samuel was shouting and waving a piece of paper in his hand. The Judge jumped up and brought his gavel down on the bench with a deafening thud. "What's the meaning of this ? He yelled "Bring those men to me at once". The policeman pushed them to the front of the court then stood back. Samuel spoke ! "I'm sorry to burst into the court like this my lord but I have something of importance to show you regarding James Maybrey".

"And why may I ask didn't you produce this before now? Said the Judge.

"Well, I've only been able to track this person down in the last hour my lord. His name is Captain Blakely he owns the good ship Victoria May docked in Liverpool". The Judge pointed to the man.

"He looks as if he's drunk, is he able to answer questions ?"

"Yes my Lord he's sober enough".

"Well man, what is it you have to say ? I haven't got all day". Samuel raised his hand and said.

"I have a document sent from a court in Kingston Jamaica that was given to this sea Captain to be delivered here to this court. It's been in his possession for nearly two weeks. It's only by shear luck that a friend of mine overheard him when he visited the shipping company. The document is an extradition order to extradite James Maybrey back to Kingston on a charge of murder". The whole court erupted in frenzy; people jumped up and down and started yelling. The Judge called for more police, and then ordered the people in the gallery to be thrown out. It took quite a while to accomplish this as they were not at all pleased. In the end the Judge had to threaten them all with jail before they finally left. While this was going on, James hung over the prisoners dock talking to his lawyer. He was furious and was waving his hands in the air. The poor lawyer didn't know what to do, he called to the Judge to allow him to read the document, but the Judge beckoned to Samuel to bring it to him. Breaking the seal he sat for a few minutes inspecting it then looked up and said.

"This document states that in March, in the year 1834 James Maybrey did unlawfully murder four African slaves who rebelled against their incarceration. The bodies were examined and found to be shot in the back. The ages of the slaves were as follows. One male aged forty two, one female aged thirty three and two children one aged twelve and the other aged thirteen" The Judge didn't get a chance to read anymore James yelled at him. "Its lies all lies, there is no proof do you here, no proof!".

"Well Mr Maybrey if you had let me finish reading the document you would have heard that there apparently were two witnesses who survived the shooting. Both are teenage boys who were hurt but escaped the onslaught. They wait in Kingston to give evidence. This is a damming evidence against you sir, and for your sake I hope you have a good alibi" James looked very white he pointed to his lawyer.

"You must give me time to talk to my lawyer, so he can examine the document. This whole thing is an outrage".

"Very well, we will have a recess for half an hour, but I must warn everybody that if there's the slightest disturbance from the benches you will all be asked to leave".

"Poor Samuel this must be so worrying for him" Elizabeth said putting her head in her hands. "I just know James is going to wiggle out of this somehow, he seems to be able to wrap everyone around this little finger".

"Well I wouldn't be so sure Elizabeth, Michael said taking her hand. The Judge can't just ignore an extradition order"

"You may be right Michael" Elizabeth said sitting up. "And maybe this time his luck will run out".

Some forty minutes later the court reassembled, the Judge addressed the lawyer.

"I hope that you and your client have had ample time to discuss this matter, and how you want to proceed. I have a lot of cases to get through today so don't waste any more time".

"I assure you my Lord this will not take long. My client wishes to say that he came to this country not as a criminal but to help his uncle a mill owner by the name of William Maybrey in the good town of Bardsley who had invited him here. Unfortunately soon after he arrived William Maybrey was lost at sea on his way back from France. As we all know this recession has hit us all badly and this mill was no exception. James Maybrey has been an asset to the community because he has kept the mill going and been able to keep most of the people of Bardsley in work. If you extradite this man it will completely devastate the town, the mill will have to be closed and the people will be thrown out of work. Surely my Lord you would have to admit this would be disastrous for our community ".

"I know of William Maybrey" said the Judge. "And his unfortunate death, he was a pillar of the community and his father before him. I'm not sure if he had any children to take over the business".

"No my Lord nobody, just a daughter, so you see this gives a different slant on the situation. Do we send him back to Jamaica to address these charges which none of us are sure are true anyway. Or do we leave him to help this community out of a bad situation, which I'm sure my Lord will understand". The Judge sat for a minute tapping his fingers on the bench. He seemed undecided, and then he addressed the court.

"At this moment in time I don't think it would be beneficial to the community to send this man back to Jamaica. I had to weigh up who would benefit most from this, and I think the people of Bardsley would benefit most, so I've had no option but to dismiss these allegations. But I will say this, that you James Maybrey have not come out of this unscathed. I'm sure in time you will be your own downfall".

James looked unmistakably relieved and thanked the Judge on behalf of the people of Bardsley. Samuel tried to intervene but to no avail. Elizabeth sat in shock, how could this happen, after all the evidence against him. She felt angry beyond belief, it was time to fight back she could almost hear her father's voice willing her to stand up.

"NO ! She shouted from the back of the court. "YOU CAN'T DO THIS TO ME; I'M THE RIGHTFUL OWNER TO MY FATHER'S ESTATE! The court went silent and the Judge pointed up to were she stood.

"Bring that girl to me at once" he said looking surprised. Before anyone could come for her Elizabeth made her way down the steps and stood in front of the court.

"Well young lady what have you to do with this case ? Speak up". Elizabeth took a deep breath and said.

"My name is Elizabeth Maybrey and I am the only beneficiary of my father's will. Ever since this man came into our lives he has dishonoured the name of Maybrey, He's miss managed my father's business, and done nothing but spend money that should have gone back into that business. My father took out a loan from the bank to pay for new steam engines to be installed at the mill to help with the production. This loan has never been paid since the day it was loaned to us" The Judge spoke to James "Is this true?"

"No my Lord, it's not true, this girl is just jealous because her father left me in charge of the mill while he left for France".

"He lies" said Elizabeth, "And what's more I can prove it" The Judge banged the gavel on his bench.

"This case is getting out of hand, do you have your father's will with you girl".

"No, my Lord I don't" Elizabeth said looking disheartened. Samuel came forward waving a paper.

"I have it my Lord I have it. It was put in my care to be delivered to her today by her lawyer. The judge took it and opened the will.

"Your father states very clearly that he wishes your cousin to look after the mill Miss Maybrey until such time as you marry. Unfortunately I can't change this as this is his last wish before he died". James slapped his hand down on the dock rail. "Thank goodness sense prevails" he said looking very smug. "The mill would not have survived by putting a slip of a girl in charge of it". Elizabeth was furious at his words; she looked over to where Michael sat, then to the judge and said. "There is something I want to tell you all my lord I was hoping to keep it secret to protect someone I love, but I have been forced to reveal it. Two nights ago I was married to a man named Michael O, Shea, in the little side chapel of my local church, where my Mother lay before her funeral. This was witnessed by Ada Woodhouse my cook and May Pierson my maid". This news sent the court wild, there were people cheering and jumping around. The judge ordered the police to quieten them down. Samuel put his arms around Elizabeth to steady her. James sat down on the seat in the dock his face ashen not knowing what to do next.

"Well young lady" said the judge, your full of surprises I must say, this changes the whole situation". He looked at the will again. "According to the will you and your husband have full control of Berkeley Mill on the day of your wedding. I am going to stand by your father's wishes and hope that you and your husband run the mill as competently as your father did. And if your father had been here today he would have been proud of the way you have handled yourself". And to Elizabeth's surprise he winked at her, she nodded to him and whispered thank you.

The judge told James to stand and said to him. "It seems your little plot has back fired on you sir, I can't say I'm particularly sorry. I'm sending you back to Jamaica with an escort to face the charges laid down in the extradition order. You will have a right to defend yourself when you get there". The judge called for him to be taken down to the cells. Elizabeth's eyes meet James's as he turned to go. All the arrogance had disappeared from them; she took no pleasure in this, just relief that she would not have to look upon him again. Samuel collected the will and they all stood up while the judge withdrew to his chambers. Michael rushed down to her and they held each other.

"I'm so proud of you " he said not wanting to let her go.

"Your not upset Michael, that I had to tell them about us ?"

"Upset ! No, I want the whole world to know that you're my wife. We don't have to hide anymore; we are free to live our lives how we want too".

"I'm so glad it's all over" she said, let's go home". They said goodbye to Samuel and Anna and thanked them for all they had done. She told them to come to dinner the following day.

The journey home seemed to take forever but finally Berkeley Grange came into view. It was a long time since Elizabeth's home resounded in such happy laughter. Even Ada was dancing around the kitchen table, her hands full of flour. It had been such a relief to be rid of a person who had made their lives a misery. The next day Elizabeth and Michael ate their breakfast in the kitchen and after eating a little too much decided to take the horses out. It was extremely hot so they took it easy and rode around the paddock for a while. Elizabeth should have been content but she felt uneasy, there was something she felt she had to do. Telling Michael to follow her she rode down towards the village. On the way they stopped to pick armfuls of spring flowers from the hedge rows. Michael knew at once where she was going with them. First stop was her Mother's grave, she lovingly replaced the old flowers with the new ones, then running her fingers over her mother's name she stood up and smiling at Michael she took his arm and walked away. All the other times she had visited the grave she had felt so depressed. But this time it was different, she felt at peace, and for the first time could turn and go without a terrible pain in her heart. It was different though, when they stood at Sharna's grave the tears were on both their cheeks. The feeling of guilt had never left Elizabeth since that fateful night. Michael sensed her grief and put his arms around her.

"You know Elizabeth, Sharna would be the last person to judge you" he said kissing her cheek. "She loved you dearly, we all harbour guilt in our hearts, but the truth is, it was not the people she loved who destroyed her".

"I'm tired of watching people suffer in this town Michael, now we have the power to change things for the better. It will be a tremendous burden for both of us, are you ready to take this enormous task on with me at your side ?"

"You have to believe me Elizabeth when I tell you that I feel the same as you about this. I've watched neighbours almost starve to death when they lost their jobs. If it hadn't been for you opening the soup kitchen like you did the death toll would have been doubled? This recession can't last forever; I'm determined to learn all I can about the business. I'll be with you every step of the way, it's our future at stake as well" Elizabeth kissed him. "Thank you; it's just what I wanted to hear. Well! There's no time like the present, we will call in at the mill and introduce you as the new owner. Mr Smithfield is in for a shock, but I'm sure he will take you under his wing and teach you everything he knows. He's a decent man and I'm sure with his help we can accomplish a lot, at least it's a start".

After they had been to the mill they went to see Michael's father. The shock was a bit to much for him comprehend; he made them repeat the news a few times before it sank in. He was so happy for his son. He kept saying how proud his mother would have been if she was alive today. They left him happier than he had ever been in his life.

As they rode up to Berkeley Grange they noticed two carriages in the drive. "That's Emily's carriage" said Elizabeth, "And the other is Samuels's I invited them to dinner tonight I'm so glad they came earlier". Michael helped her down from her horse. "I'll stable the horses for you Elizabeth, you go and greet your guests I'll come to the house later". As she entered the drawing room Emily ran to her.

"My darling Elizabeth are you alright ? Father told me all what you have been through, I wish you would have asked us to help you earlier. I can't imagine how you must have suffered because of that awful man".

"How did your Father know about this ? Asked Elizabeth bewildered.

"Well my Father and Samuel went looking for this terrible sea captain fellow. It took a long time to find him. They must have searched nearly every tavern in Manchester.

"I didn't know you went to so much trouble Samuel, Elizabeth said . I owe you so much, please except my thanks for what you have done for us".

"There's no need to thank me child, it was just lucky that when our captain visited the shipping company he let slip about the extradition papers and who they where for. My good friend who works there knew your Father, and told me about it".

"But how did the police in Jamaica know where he had gone ?"

"He must have bragged about the position he obtained in England, it was his undoing" Emily wagged a finger at Elizabeth. "You are naughty getting married behind my back, I thought I was going to beat you to the alter" she said laughing.

"I'm afraid I had to bring my wedding forward Emily to bring this unfortunate business to a final conclusion. I will be having a formal wedding soon as the other one was not strictly legal as the bands where not put up in the church but as you can see my little ploy worked" she said laughing.

"Why you little minx" Emily said hugging her. What a clever ploy, I don't suppose you would consider a double wedding; Edward and I would be honoured if you would say yes".

"I think that's a lovely idea Emily, thank you. Michael and I would love to accept your offer, I think he would be less nervous if Edward was there with him".

"It's settled then; I must go and tell everyone the good news. We will see you tonight for dinner; we can talk about the weddings then. And Elizabeth, about Michael, once it gets around he has been accepted socially into our home other people will accept him too and I do so want you to be happy".

"That is really sweet of you Emily I promise to bring him to Arlington Hall soon when we are more settled".

After she said goodbye to Emily Elizabeth rang for some tea for herself and Samuel. It was a good few hours till dinner so they chatted and waited for Michael to arrive.

"Did Anna not wish to come to dinner Samuel asked Elizabeth, I was looking forward to seeing you both"?

"I wanted to talk to you and Michael alone tonight my dear, I have something to say that has been on my mind for so long".

"My, that sounds intriguing, I can't wait to hear about it, well now is the time I hear his footsteps in the hallway". Michael entered with a big smile on his face.

"Sorry I'm late, I had to help John settle the horses down, has Emily gone ? I was hoping to see her".

"I'm sorry you missed her" Elizabeth said patting the seat next to her for him to sit. "She had to go, but she invited us to Monkford Hall we will go next week.

Samuel went to the drinks cupboard and poured himself a drink, then just stood with his back to them not saying anything. Michael whispered to Elizabeth. "Is there anything wrong ? She put her finger to her lips as if to say don't say anything. Samuel turned and said to them.

"What I'm about to say has been on my mind for a long time. If your Father and Mother where alive Elizabeth this conversation I'm about to have with you would never be taking place. I swore to your Mamma that what I am about to tell you would never come to light. That was before you lost them both". Elizabeth looked bewildered but didn't say anything.

"I told you the other day that you're Mamma and I wanted to marry before she meet your Father. Unfortunately her Father wouldn't allow it, so we parted. Two years later she married your Father. I'm quite convinced that she loved him, perhaps in a different way than the feelings we had together. Later on in the marriage she found herself more and more unhappy and losing her children didn't help. And your Father sensing this buried himself in his work, she never hardly saw him as he was always at the mill. I saw how distressed she was and tried to help. We went on long rides in the carriage and sometimes she visited me at home. As you can guess we had a brief affair. I'm not proud of what I did, and it was over almost as quickly as it began" Elizabeth just sat in shock not being able to speak. Michael put his arms around her. "Are you all right" he said looking worried she nodded. "I have a feeling you have more to tell us Samuel, please say what you have to say, I don't want Elizabeth distressed anymore than she has to be". Samuel shook his head. "I'm sorry

Elizabeth if I've upset you, but you have a right to know that I am in fact your real Father. Your Mamma begged me not to reveal this as it would have destroyed her in the eyes of the community. We didn't know how your Father would react. All I cared about at the time was protecting your Mamma. When she revealed that she was with child she told me the child was mine, I know it was a cowardly thing not to tell your Father but your Mamma's happiness was all I wanted so we said nothing. I hope you can forgive me, but I'll understand if you can't, please say something". Elizabeth walked to the door wiping her eyes and said she was going for a walk, Michael followed her. He helped her on with her cloak and they left the house. They walked for a couple of minutes Michael waiting for her to speak.

"It's all been a lie hasn't it" she said with tears running down her cheeks." I thought I knew my parents but it seems I didn't know them at all. How could Mamma have lived a lie all these years? I had a right to know didn't I ?"

"Elizabeth you judge your Mamma to harshly, just think if this had got out. She could have been ostracized from the community. What I do believe is she was protecting her child; this sort of thing is not looked upon as being acceptable. Just think of what your Mamma must have gone through, knowing she had done this to your Father, and having to keep this secret all these years. By what you have told me she seems to have been a gentle person who perhaps had difficulty standing up to your Father, is that how you see it ?"

"You're right of cause that's just how it's been" she said wiping her eyes." But Father had his good points too; he made sure we had every comfort. We had a good life here when most people of this town were going hungry. It was only a short while ago that I saw things as they really are. My troubles are nothing compared to those people".

"Do you think your Mamma would have told you eventually, if she had lived ?"
"Yes I'm quite sure she would have if my Father had died first. She was a wonderful Mother and a good friend. I can't be angry at someone whom I loved, it's just been a shock that's all. Do you realise Michael that James may have been the rightful

owner of Berkeley Grange after all, and he didn't even realise it "

"That man didn't deserve to inherit anything Elizabeth, don't tell me you feel bad about it?"

"No of cause not he got what he deserved".

"What are your feelings towards Samuel now, has this changed your opinion towards him?"

"If I'm honest with myself, my feelings haven't changed at all, he's a wonderful person in every respect I admire and love him. He must have loved Mamma so much and he never found anyone to replace her".

"You know Elizabeth this poor man waits in your drawing room wondering if you are going to tell him to leave or except him into your life. He's not getting any younger, and you can tell by the way he looks at you that he loves you very much". Elizabeth took Michael's hand.

"My poor, poor Samuel I must go to him, I couldn't hurt that dear man if I tried".

"I'm so glad you said that" Michael said with relief, I was scared in case you wouldn't forgive him".

"I think it's time for forgiveness all round Michael. I lost my Family in a matter of months and gained another. How many people can say that"? Michael kissed her gently. "Come on Elizabeth it's time for us to start living, the past will have to wait. We have a long hard road ahead, are you ready ?" Smiling at him Elizabeth kissed him back. "I can't wait" Turning they made their way back to the Manor and to their future.

END

****